"I'm sorry, Raine."

Cotter rolled away from her, not stopping until he was hunched on the edge of the bed. Pulling the sheet about her body, she could only stare wide-eyed as he looked up and stared unseeing out the window. "Professor Raine Webber. Sweet, book-smart, earnest, protected and protective. You're delicate, Raine, too delicate for a man like me. What do I have to offer you? There are rules about what a man like me can do—how far I can go with a woman..."

Her lips began to tremble but she began, "Cotter, I don't know who you think I am or what this means to us."

"Damn!" He grabbed her pajamas, lying rumpled on the floor. With self-disgust in his face, he tossed them at her. "What I'm saying is I'm no Prince Charming...and I have no intentions of becoming one!"

ABOUT THE AUTHOR

Renee Roszel feels that a combination of writing and aerobic dance, which she teaches part-time, provides a very even balance in her life. She started writing as a journalism major in college. After getting married and raising two sons, she dabbled in advertising, but ultimately came back to her true love—writing. Renee now resides in Tulsa, Oklahoma, with her family.

Books by Renee Roszel

HARLEQUIN AMERICAN ROMANCE

10—HOSTAGE HEART
129—ANOTHER MAN'S TREASURE

These books may be available at your local bookseller.

Don't miss any of our special offers. Write to us at the following address for information on our newest releases.

Harlequin Reader Service
P.O. Box 52040, Phoenix, AZ 85072-2040
Canadian address: P.O. Box 2800, Postal Station A,
5170 Yonge St., Willowdale, Ont. M2N 6J3

Another Man's Treasure
RENEE ROSZEL

Harlequin Books

TORONTO • NEW YORK • LONDON
AMSTERDAM • PARIS • SYDNEY • HAMBURG
STOCKHOLM • ATHENS • TOKYO • MILAN

To Norda,
for all the times I pinched her and made her cry.

Published December 1985

First printing October 1985

ISBN 0-373-16129-8

Copyright © 1985 by Renee Roszel. All rights reserved.
Philippine copyright 1985. Australian copyright 1985.
Except for use in any review, the reproduction or utilization of
this work in whole or in part in any form by any electronic,
mechanical or other means, now known or hereafter invented,
including xerography, photocopying and recording, or in any
information storage or retrieval system, is forbidden without
the permission of the publisher, Harlequin Enterprises Limited,
225 Duncan Mill Road, Don Mills, Ontario, Canada M3B 3K9.

All the characters in this book have no existence outside the
imagination of the author and have no relation whatsoever to
anyone bearing the same name or names. They are not even
distantly inspired by any individual known or unknown to the
author, and all the incidents are pure invention.

The Harlequin trademarks, consisting of the words
HARLEQUIN AMERICAN ROMANCE, HARLEQUIN
AMERICAN ROMANCES, and the portrayal of a Harlequin,
are trademarks of Harlequin Enterprises Limited; the portrayal
of a Harlequin is registered in the United States Patent and
Trademark Office and in the Canada Trade Marks Office.

Printed in Canada

Chapter One

A white mansion framed by branches of sprawling sugar maples, pines and elms caught Raine's eye. The warm June sun cast a patchwork of shadows across its face, drawing conflicting sharp lines beneath overhanging eaves and behind columns and cornices. Yet as Raine's middle-aged station wagon approached along the meandering coast road, the grand house's face softened. Green-swathed branches, caught in a cool sea breeze, beckoned toward her, suggesting mutely that she detour from her planned route and explore its hidden recesses and towering galleries. With regret, she drew her eyes away to maneuver her car around a sharp curve in the road.

"Oh! Turn here, Miss Webber." Nordie Hunt, wedged between two male students in the backseat, sat forward, pointing. "That's our house."

Raine guided the car around the bend and blinked into the rearview mirror. "Where?"

"That white house." Nordie gestured toward the mansion Raine had just been admiring. "That's Hunt's Treasure. See, there's the gate."

Raine did see. Heavens, she'd had no idea that Nordie's family lived in Portland, in a mansion that was Maine's answer to Scarlett O'Hara's Tara! She'd expected the president of Scavenger Hunt, Inc. to have a nice home, but this? Turning off the main road, she stopped her car before a gate, an impressive structure ten feet tall. It was a well-wrought work of art, with the initial "H" swirled in script amid delicate metal leaves and vines. Massive brick pillars flanked the elaborate metalwork.

"Roll down the window, Bill," Nordie instructed the redhead that sat beside her. "I'll get us in."

Nordie leaned across him and waited.

"May I ask your business?" The crusty voice was especially startling, since it was amplified by a speaker in the brick pillar.

"Hi, Lys. It's me, Nordie. I'm in a station wagon and there's another car behind me. Let us in, will you?"

"Yes, ma'am." There was a pause. "Good to have you home."

"Thanks." Raine watched her attractive student in the side-view mirror, noticing the slight frown that appeared on the pert young face. "Say, Lys, is Cotter home, or in town?"

"Home. In his office."

"Okay. Better tell him we're here." She sounded vaguely doubtful.

"Yes, ma'am."

"Oh, and Lys? How's Carl?"

There was another pause before the crackly voice replied, "He is about the same, ma'am."

"Oh." The word was a disappointed sigh. "Okay, Lys. Thanks."

"You're welcome, ma'am."

The gate slowly swung open, allowing them to enter the private grounds. A narrow drive curved along the manicured lawn, leading them to the three-story manse.

As Bill rolled up the window, Nordie settled back in her seat. "Professor Webber, I figure we'll be able to do the cataloguing in the building that used to be the stables." She waved toward the side of the house, and Raine observed a long, low brick building with six arched entries. Nordie seemed enthusiastic again as she explained, "It's empty now, so there's plenty of room to back a truck inside, and lots of flat surfaces where we can set up tables. I think it'll be okay."

Raine smiled at the understatement. "It sounds perfect." She wondered at Nordie's matter-of-fact attitude. Raine had known her student for only one semester. She was a friendly kid and an adequate worker when she applied herself. But nothing she'd mentioned had given Raine an inkling of the vast wealth Nordie's family commanded. Perhaps that was how it was with people who had always known wealth; they took it completely for granted.

She pulled the car up in front of the towering house only seconds before the excited team of students began pouring from every door. Just as she grabbed the strap of her shoulder bag and stepped from the car, she heard Nordie cry delightedly, "Cotter! Oh, Cot!" Raine closed the door and paused, careful to stay out of Nordie's path as she scurried toward one of the staircases leading to the majestic porch.

About halfway up the wide steps, a man was waiting. In white shirt and slacks, he looked very much like one of the house's pillars, and almost as immovable. As Nordie charged up the steps, Raine guessed that he was Cotter Hunt, their host. Tall and trim, he stood motionless, his silver hair glistening in the noon sun. Raine watched his face as he scanned the group of eight male students milling between the cars before his eyes settled on Raine. She swallowed at his expression. Despite his strong, open features, he seemed tense. She became uneasy as his black eyes regarded her. But his scrutiny was brief; an instant later, his attention was drawn from her to Nordie as she leapt into her brother's arms.

"Oh, Cot! I'm so glad to see you." She wrapped her arms about his neck. Raine watched as he folded Nordie into a familiar embrace.

Raine heard a deep, resonant voice and realized it was Cotter talking to Nordie. Nordie had assured her that all had been arranged, but now she was not so sure. Could it be that Nordie's request to bring Raine and her group there might have actually been refused, and in her eagerness she had ignored the rejection and brought them anyway? Raine nervously adjusted her glasses, squinting to get a better look at Cotter's face. He wasn't exactly frowning, but he didn't look delighted, either. Nordie was speaking now, her gestures animated, her voice low.

"Oh, Lord." Raine exhaled slowly in a practiced effort to keep cool. She watched the man shake his head, indicating something far from promising perhaps? She should have known it was too good to be true. And she shouldn't have let Nordie insist on making all the arrangements herself. But knowing that *now* wasn't especially helpful....

Hearing a scraping sound behind her, Raine turned to see the boys pulling bags from the trunk of the second car. She was about to caution them to wait a few moments when Nordie called down to them. "Well, aren't you all going to come on up and meet my big brother?"

Raine turned to see both of them watching the group. Cotter's hands were clasped around the marble railing, and Nordie had circled one of his arms with hers.

The boys grabbed their gear and began to hurry up the wide steps. Still feeling unsure of the situation, Raine smoothed the wrinkles out of her navy skirt and followed the boys.

"First, Cot," Nordie announced, motioning toward the group, "I want you to meet my anthropology professor, Miss Raine Webber." She waved the young men back like a mother hen, and they automatically made a path for Raine to precede them. "She's going to lead this dig."

Cotter lifted one arched brow, his lips curling into a half smile. It was more an expression of curiosity than greeting. He held out his hand, and as Raine accepted it she was struck by how nicely manicured it was. Odd, she thought, considering his business. Clearing her throat, she spoke first. "Hello, Mr. Hunt."

He murmured her title, "Professor." In the back of her mind it occurred to her that his hand felt warm, making hers seem strangely cold.

Their contact was brief and businesslike, but the warmth of his hand lingered. She offered quietly, "Please, call me Raine."

"You're too kind." The remark seemed cynical but the half smile remained.

In the awkward pause that followed, she cleared her throat again, almost afraid to broach the subject of why they were there. This introduction might just be his preamble to telling her—however politely—to take her pack of pupils back to the University of Maine and leave him and his wayward sister their privacy.

Her natural shyness made it even harder to look into Cotter's dark eyes. But Raine quietly urged herself to confront him, at least to clarify his position on the project. *You might as well get it over with,* she reasoned. *He's either going to tell you to get out, or he isn't!* With a forced smile, she tried to sound upbeat. "You were very kind to allow us to come here to do our garbology study. When Nordie told me about your firm and your offer to help, I was...overwhelmed." She immediately regretted her choice of words. The situation didn't call for superlatives.

"Yes, well, it is somewhat overwhelming, isn't it?" His expression didn't change.

Was that a yes or a no? Her smile began to fade.

Before she had time to put the question into words, he added, "How my operation can possibly be worth an anthropologist's time is a mystery to me, professor...Raine, but I would never stand in the path of Nordie's education, no matter how bizarre and convoluted that path might become."

Relieved by his positive answer, Raine nodded in response. But her curiosity of Cotter's diffident manner increased.

With a flashing sidelong look at his sister, Cotter turned to Raine and spoke in a confidential tone.

"Nordie's been a bit vague about the details; perhaps we can discuss your exact needs later today at dinner." His smile was evident now, but somehow it seemed superficial, almost like a public relations device. "Meanwhile, I'm sure Nordie would love to show you around the grounds while I tell Hanna to get your rooms ready." He turned toward his sister, adding, "We weren't expecting you quite this early."

Nordie coughed into her hand, and Raine was sure she saw the trace of a smile diminish before Nordie spoke. "Great idea, Cot. I'll introduce you to these trash diggers at dinner." Turning to the young men, she tossed her head toward the ocean. "Let's go down to the beach for a while. Professor Webber, you come, too. Lys'll get the bags."

"Okay." Raine hesitated a moment and glanced at the porch in time to see Cotter Hunt disappear around one of the columns. The echo of a heavy door opening and closing marked his exit.

Her thoughts remained on Cotter as she wondered about the guarded, quiet man. He seemed to be thirty-five or forty and he shared the sculpted features of his young sister. But there was a striking difference between brother and sister: Cotter's eyes had a distracted quality, and they were darker than Nordie's. His expression seemed to lack the amusement of his sister's. In fact, his eyes held no laughter at all. Instead, they revealed an intriguing hint of wariness, like a hunted—or haunted—creature.

"Professor?" Raine felt Nordie's hand on her wrist, and turned toward the younger woman. It was very quiet now, and Raine realized that the young men had headed down the steps and were on their way toward the beach.

"Yes?"

Nordie made an excessive point of looking in every direction before whispering conspiratorially, "I—I thought you ought to know." She paused, making sure that she had her teacher's undivided attention before adding in a rush, "I—I thought you ought to know. My brother—Cotter—is gay."

BENT STUDIOUSLY over his huge mahogany desk, Cotter made an entry in his account book, "You told who what, Nordie?" He inclined his head to look at her as he sat back in the red leather wing chair.

She pouted, a flicker of humor evident in her brown eyes as she veered away from the subject. "You know, Cotter, I should be the beautiful one, not you."

"You should be committed." His expression was loving, if slightly skeptical.

She laughed. "Oh, but I am. I am. Totally."

"To what? Getting me committed? Nine house guests without any advance warning—for a month, yet? I should thrash you to within an inch of your life." He held the gold pen between his long fingers, remarking with a casualness that he knew would thoroughly irk her, "Should I expect a busload of psychiatrists to arrive later today for a live-in study of your demented sense of humor?"

At her exasperated humph his smile broadened, and he shook his head. Cotter loved his sister to a fault. Unfortunately for Cotter, she knew it.

He couldn't help the way he felt about her. She was an unpredictable kid, spoiled and petted because he'd done everything in his power to protect her from the harshness of the world he had known as a child. And, to be truthful, he was happy that she had no memory of the hard times. He'd given everything he could afford to give—both to her and to his younger brother, Carl. He wanted them to have everything they might have had if their parents had lived—if he, in his cowardice, hadn't failed to save them from their burning house trailer. It was his fault that they had been left alone, without parents. Nordie and Carl were his only family, and he had made his promise to be their guardian twenty years ago.

With a wry grin at her expression of practiced innocence, he asked more seriously, "Why do you take so much delight in doing these things to me?"

"Why did Pike climb the peak?"

He pursed his lips. "I didn't think it was to irritate his brother."

"Of course not, Cotter. It was for the challenge, the excitement!" She stuck out her lower lip. "Actually, surprising you with Professor Webber *et al* wasn't as much fun as I'd hoped it would be. You recovered too quickly. I don't think they even realized you didn't know they were coming." She lifted a warning finger and eyed him menacingly. "But I'll trip up that calm facade of yours yet."

"Heaven help me when that day comes." He closed the book and dropped the pen into his top drawer. "Now what were you saying before? You told who what?"

Her lips twitched. "I said, I told Professor Webber you're gay."

He heard her that time. At least he thought he heard her. With any luck at all, his hearing was going, and she'd actually said she'd told Professor Webber that he was gray. That was true—obvious, but true; or maybe she'd meant tht he was happily excited, which, at the moment, was only half true—if you could call apoplexy being excited. He shuddered inwardly. His smile had frozen and was now melting into a grim line. "What?" The rasped whisper grated with disbelief. "You told Professor Webber I'm..." His powerfully built shoulders hunched as he slammed his palms on the desk surface to catapult himself to his feet. The chair, knocked off balance, hit by the back of his legs, slammed into the wall with the force.

Nordie jumped in reaction to the booming sound, but her wide eyes remained riveted. Cotter's strong, tanned features had turned to stone, and his face had taken on a disquieting pallor when he reached his full height of six feet three inches.

"There's not much I'd put past you, Nora Diane Hunt, but please tell me you didn't."

She was squinting, trying to read his lips. He had spoken very quietly, afraid to do more. When she nodded, his anger was suddenly too strong to conceal, and he curled his hands into knotted fists. This time his baby sister had gone too far with her practical joking.

Years and years of saying and doing the most outrageous things had come and gone as she'd played the game of trying to get Cotter angry; years of half victories and partial wins. But, if Nordie was telling him the truth, she had outdone herself this time. He was incensed and no longer had the strength to repress his feelings.

Her smile was inquisitive. Blinking wide, innocent eyes, she prodded, "Cot, why is your jaw throbbing like that?" The question was high-pitched. "Did I getcha? Did I actually find your Achilles' heel? The Machismo Syndrome?"

He growled, taking a step toward her, and she took a step backward. When he didn't speak, she tried one of her remember-you-love-me-no-matter-what-I've-done smiles and held up a placating hand. "Lighten up, Cotter. Just give me a minute to explain. I had to tell her that."

He looked at her as though she were a maniac. "You told a perfect stranger—a guest in our house—that your brother is gay?" As soon as the word was out of his mouth, he clamped his jaw shut and with narrowed eyes glanced at the entrance to the den. The doors were closed; nevertheless, he lowered his voice. "Damn it, Nordie! Why?"

She opened her mouth, but he halted her words with a shake of the head. "This had better be good, or it will be the last thing you explain on this earth."

"Cotter, Cotter," she said, "would I say such a thing without a good reason?"

He snorted. "Do paranoids look over their shoulders?"

"I'm sure I don't know," she answered, looking wounded. Squaring her shoulders, she charged on. "You're too damned handsome. That's why I told her you're gay."

He stared, dumbfounded, unable to fathom her ludicrous remark. Apparently his silence gave her new courage. He watched in shock as her lips lifted in the practiced smile of a coquette. Walking toward her brother, she took his hand. "It was for Carl," she purred up at him. "He's been so down ever since he was hurt at spring training. I mean his whole life was being quarterback for the Patriots, and now he may never walk again." She squeezed his hand and looked up lovingly, and to his astonishment, she even managed to look a little pitiful. "And on top of everything, Carl's wife walking out on him like that. Can't you see why I had to do it?"

Answering her with sarcasm, he countered, "Of course. It's all as clear as mud."

Nordie couldn't contain a laugh. "Actually, I told Professor Webber that you were gay 'cause I wanted her to pay attention to Carl while she's here. She's a Patriots fan, and—" she grinned at him again "—remember the saleslady that kept coming to our door week after week, trying to sell you siding?"

His black brows furrowed in extreme irritation. "So? What does that have to do with anything?"

"So, we were living in an apartment at the time, remember? I may not be the brightest person in the world, but I *have* figured out the effect you have on women."

"You were eight years old then."

"But you were twenty-five and you attracted women like bees to honey. To be honest, I don't see why." She rolled her eyes as though hopelessly confused by it all. "But facts are facts."

"Thanks so much!" He was disgusted with her, and he made no effort to restrain his pointed question. "But didn't you forget one particularly significant fact?"

"I don't think so, no."

He bared his teeth. "Oh, no? How about the fact that I'm not gay? That's not significant?"

She waved his argument aside as though it were useless trivia. "Oh, Cotter, don't get so uptight. Only insecure men have to prove their masculinity all the time." Lifting a coy shoulder, she inquired softly, "Don't you want to help Carl snap out of his depression?"

Cotter felt himself falling for Nordie's childish but heartfelt argument. Sometimes he hated the way that kid had always been able to wrap him around her little finger—never more than now, however.

"Isn't Carl's mental health and happiness worth a month of being 'womanless'? Especially since your current lady friend is out of town?"

"What about my mental health? The woman's going to be looking at me as if I were Typhoid Mary."

"Cotter Hunt! After all these years, you're not suddenly going to become selfish and self-centered, are you?" She planted her hands on her hips. He noticed that one sandaled foot had begun tapping with impatience. "Besides, Professor Webber isn't your type—much too scholarly. So where's the problem?" She reached up and patted his cheek. "Anyway, you've got enough mental health for both of us. You can handle a little shunning by a college professor for your brother, can't you?"

He groaned. "A little shunning, she calls it."

"But you will do it—for Carl?" She grasped his wrist. "You'll be gay around Professor Webber?"

"Not gay, maybe mildly pleasant." He released himself and looked up at the ceiling. "Damn it, Nordie. I ought to tell the woman you're a pathological liar." He leveled his gaze on her again. "It would serve you right."

"Oh, please don't tell her, Cotter! My God, she'd flunk me on the spot!"

"So?" He lifted a dark brow. "Last semester you were a music history major. What happened to your burning passion for Bach and the cronies?"

"Oh, uh—" she twitched her shoulders nervously "—he got married."

"Bach?"

"No, Ken McCardy! He was a gorgeous senior—a violinist."

"Ah!" Cotter nodded with an exaggerated expression of understanding. "So much for higher education. Who's your target this time? I presume he's part of the invasion you brought with you this afternoon."

She blushed. "Bill. The tall redhead. But, you're getting us off the subject."

"I was certainly trying."

"Oh, Cotter, don't be that way. Remember, it's not just one of my better pranks. It's for Carl." The tremulous note of pleading in her voice was meant to fuel her argument, he knew. "Besides," she was continuing, "if Professor Webber is anything like ordinary women, in twenty-four hours she'll be chasing after you, worshiping you. She'd be in your way all the time."

His lips quirked. She was outrageous, but she was his sister. "You fling a mean piece of garbage."

"You will do this, won't you?"

He looked at her, his brow wrinkling as he grew serious. "You know this whole scheme is ridiculous."

She bit her lower lip and looked toward the floor, nodding. "Uh-huh." Her humility seemed genuine.

"You realize you're asking more of me than you have any right to."

She only nodded, but this time she clasped her hands behind her back.

"You understand that if anyone else asked this of me I'd tell him—or *her*—to forget it."

She turned a trustful gaze toward him. "You're going to do it—for Carl, aren't you?" It wasn't a question.

Carl. Cotter pictured his pale, desperately depressed brother as he had been since the operation a month ago. The prognosis had been fair, but Carl had decided it was hopeless. When he had slipped to his lowest point, Cammie, his wife of five years had simply left. The pressure of consoling Carl, of helping him with the loss of his football career and self-esteem, had been too much for her.

Carl seemed to have lost his interest in everything during the past weeks. Yes, Carl needed something to spark his interest in living again. Maybe a woman—a fan—just might be a new beginning for him. He didn't really see the necessity of this charade, but it was done now, and anything he did to undo it could only hurt Nordie. She might deserve the reprimand she would get from her teacher, but he couldn't do it to her. Besides, as Nordie had said, he wasn't interested in the woman anyway. With a sense of resolve he finalized their plan. "Four weeks?"

"Yes."

"Do I have to wave a hankie?"

Her eyes lit up. "Would you?"

"No."

She grimaced. "That's what I thought."

"No one else can know. Not Bill the redhead or any of the others. Just your professor."

"Oh, Cot! Oh, thank you!" she gasped, hugging him to her. "You won't regret this when you see how Carl brightens up. I think he and Miss Webber are out on the terrace by the pool talking right now. She's just what he needs. You wait and see. He'll be so much better with someone around to admire him."

Cotter allowed her to crush him against her only until she paused to catch her breath. Then, disengaging himself, he placed a quieting hand on her shoulder. "Don't do anything like this again. You know how important it is to me that you get an education. So I won't show you up to be the hopeless practical joker you are. But don't press your luck. If it weren't for Carl, I'd just let people know about the kinds of things you concentrate on and have you learn the hard way."

She smiled even in the face of his stern resolve. "Like you did?"

He shook his head at her reminder of how he had started, nearly twenty-one years ago. "I had the damned dirt under my nails for years. Maybe I got my money that way, but not respect. I want you to have that, Nordie—you and Carl." His eyes were clouded with memory when they found hers again. Muttering more to himself than to her, he added, "You don't get respect riding a garbage truck, you get that with an education. And, damn it, Nordie, you're going to have it."

She blinked back tears, whispering in an unsteady voice, "I may not end up an anthropologist, Cotter. But I promise you I'll get the education, for myself and for...all of us."

He grunted approvingly. She hugged him to her. "What a wonderful brother you are. How wonderful and tough and sensitive."

She sniffled, mumbling into his chest, "I know I give you trouble sometimes, Cot, but I'm awfully proud of the orphaned kid who swung onto the back of that garbage truck and kept his screaming baby sister and ten-year-old brother clothed and fed. And I'll tell anybody who'll listen how you turned Scavenger Hunt, Incorporated, into a profitable trash-refining company—a model in the industry." She looked up at him, her eyes swimming with proud tears. "I mean, how many other refuse companies offer shares to their workers? And how many other companies are turning a landfill into a park with a methane gas plant that will increase Portland's energy supply while lowering the cost? You tell me, Cotter? How many?"

He frowned, knowing she wouldn't be so proud of him if she knew the truth about why they were orphans. He shook his head, his arms tightening about her for a silent moment before letting her go. "Why don't you go tell your Professor Webber to round up the troop. I think Hanna should have their rooms ready by now."

She reached up and grazed his chin with a kiss. "Okay. See you later."

"And while you're getting them settled, I'll go change for dinner." His voice was neutral, but Nordie could tell he was no longer angry. Some things were important, and some weren't. And to Cotter, there was nothing more important than his family.

Chapter Two

Raine closed the door of the room that Nordie had given to her. In a state of shock, she looked around. It was massive, decorated for a man, in gold and brown tones suggesting understated elegance. The king-size bed, covered by a sleek gold spread, was set in an unusually luxurious wood frame. An armoire and chest of the same wood flanked the bed. Behind a row of throw pillows on the bed Raine could see a leather-cushioned headrest. The wall behind was a subtle brown and burnished gold.

Brass pots and lacquered wicker baskets of various sizes filled with plants were scattered about the room, complementing the sleekness of the furnishings. Under the long window, covered by drapes of the same lustrous fabric as the spread, was a beautifully proportioned window seat, overlooking the garden.

An oak mirror dominated the wall opposite the window. It was of the same rich wood as the other pieces. With a casual brush of her fingers through her short hair, she peered at herself. It had been a long drive, caravaning down east from the university with Nordie and her friends. She was tired and felt she could have been more articulate when she'd been introduced to Cotter and his ailing brother.

She began to unbutton her blouse but frowned at her reflection. Why had Nordie told her such an intimate fact about Cotter? For that matter, she couldn't imagine any man telling his sister such a thing. But then, she wasn't in charge of how people thought and what they did. What was said was said, and it was certainly none of her business. She shook her head. Raine had never been eager to fault people because of their differences. Certainly, she'd learned that the hard way, being labeled "different" most of her life. First, as a child, before she'd had her eye surgery, she'd been cross-eyed. Then, she'd been called Four Eyes and later The Brain. She knew how it felt to be the object of ridicule. Even now, at thirty-four, she'd occasionally heard herself referred to as "that old-maid schoolteacher."

It was because of this labeling Raine had silently endured that she was especially sensitive. As she pulled the blouse over her head, she vowed that Cotter's secret would be safe with her, and that she would do everything in her power to keep the situation comfortable while she and her students were there. He'd certainly seemed ill at ease when they'd arrived. He probably spent too much of his life feeling uneasy.

She looked at her watch. It was nearly six. Nordie had said that dinner would be at seven. Good. That would give her time to wash away the road dust and change. She hoped her students would do the same. She was their teacher, not their mother. But most of them seemed acquainted with the etiquette of being a guest. And Nordie was an outgoing person. Surely, she would let them know the house rules. Raine smiled at the thought of Nordie's luminous personality. She bubbled all the time.

Raine's eyes met her reflection in the mirror. Behind the big square frames, her brown eyes were huge, somber windows to her shy soul. The smile faded. How she wished she could be more sociable. She had to fight her shyness continuously. A college professor, in her mind, shouldn't be shy. But really making contact with others was hard work for someone who had spent a good deal of her time alone.

Slipping off her pearl earrings, she swept the short brown hair away from her face, brushing the curved strands behind her ears. Mumbling to herself, she cajoled, "Cotter Hunt will be good practice for you, Raine. You can work at being outgoing by making him your friend. Lord knows, he probably needs a friend."

Funny. She pulled off her glasses and began to slip out of her skirt. He didn't look anything like the stereotype of a gay man. But then, there really wasn't such a thing as an incarnation of a stereotype. If Nordie hadn't mentioned it, Raine would never have guessed. With a sigh, again wishing Nordie hadn't shared this information with her, she carried her clothing to the closet. She was surprised to see that someone had already hung up her other things. She smiled. It was certainly wonderful of Cotter to allow all of them to come here and stay while they conducted their project with his collection company.

She turned away from the closet, scanning the room again. Now that she was actually here, the accommodations filled her with a new disbelief that this could really be happening. They were staying, free of charge, in a mansion by the sea! It certainly wasn't an experience most college professors encountered in their everyday lives.

One of the features of Raine's life was that she was invariably early for everything. It was still only six forty-five, and she couldn't bear to just sit on the edge of her bed waiting for the dinner hour.

Deciding she would probably not be committing a mortal sin by appearing downstairs, she put aside the book she'd been trying to read. She stood, smoothing the beige linen of her shirtdress as she slipped her feet into open-toed pumps. With one last sweep of her fingers through her hair, she headed out the door and down the curving staircase toward the entry hall. Halfway down, she halted, straining to hear the music emanating from behind a set of double doors. She recognized the recording immediately. It was a jazz classic of Thelonious Monk.

Curious, she hurried down the rest of the steps and headed toward the room. One of the doors stood slightly ajar. She hesitated to peek inside; it might be impudent of her to look further. But she was a jazz fan. Her curiosity about the other jazz enthusiast among them made her pull the door wide enough to peer in.

The room was dark, except for the fading light of a dying day that filtered in through the leaded glass windows. Movement in a chair behind a large desk caught her attention, and she squinted in that direction. Her eyes were slow to adjust to the dimness, and she couldn't make out the figure. Clearing her throat nervously, she called over the music. "I'm sorry to disturb you. I—just wondered who else liked The Monk." She still wondered, unable to identify the person who was sitting in the shadows.

"Come in, professor."

The voice answered her inquiry. It was Cotter. Surprised to hear him refer to her by her title, she wondered if it had something to do with his feeling for women in general. It was probably his way of keeping his distance.

She felt apprehensive about seeing him—facing him—since she knew intimate information about him without really knowing him. But she straightened her shoulders, silently encouraging herself to overcome timidity. Face the man, and make him her friend. After all, his kindness in allowing them these extravagant accommodations warranted some form of friendliness. And if that friendliness required additional effort on her part, then so be it. She stepped inside and pulled the door to the same position it had been before she had opened it. "Hello, Cotter. I hope you'll forgive my intrusion, but I haven't heard ''Round about Midnight' in years."

He swiveled his chair around to face her. The first thing she could see was the glint of his silver hair. As her eyes became more accustomed to the darkness, she began to observe the contours of his face. He was frowning. Or was that merely his look of curiosity? He asked quietly, "Why? Did he fall out of favor with you?"

She smiled. That wasn't the question she'd expected. "No. It's because the last time my folks moved, a box of my favorite records was lost in the shipping. But I'll never forget it. Mother collected everything The Monk recorded—along with Miles Davis, Milt Jackson—you name it. If it was jazz, and if it was ever recorded, we had it."

"I thought you were a football fan."

She lifted her chin questioningly. "How did you know I was a football fan?"

"Nordie."

She laughed. "Oh, yes. Well, I am. And a jazz fan, too. My dad was a football coach at a small midwestern university until he retired a few years ago. Mom taught piano. Her hobby was playing jazz piano—still is."

She thought she heard a quiet 'Hmm,' but she wasn't sure. The music had ended, and the room had fallen into deep silence. The leather creaked, and a tall silhouette moving before the window told her that he was going to play it again. "Would you like to sit down and hear the whole thing?" He adjusted the needle on the stereo and turned to face her.

"Why yes, thanks."

He walked back to the desk and flipped on a small reading lamp. Light changed the complexion of the room entirely. It went from formless and forbidding to rich and warm, a tasteful blend of earthy colors. The walls were paneled with wood, deeply colored and well oiled. Directly opposite the desk was a wall entirely covered with shelves filled with books. A Navaho-type woven rug reflected the autumn tones of the other furniture and covered the maple wood floor.

As the music began, she was still standing. Cotter seemed to sense her hesitation, and he nodded toward a couch beside the double doors. "The music sounds best from there."

After taking the suggested seat, she was surprised to see him coming to join her. There was plenty of room, but she backed into the throw pillow on her end anyway.

Leaning an elbow on the arm of the couch, she offered, "You're right about the music. I feel as though The Monk is right here in the room. Your sound system is wonderful."

"My acoustics consultant will be happy to hear that." He sat down at the other end, laying his arm casually across the back of the couch. Even with the long fingers stretched toward her, he was still a good distance away from her. As he watched her face, she wondered what he saw—besides the glasses. She hoped he couldn't see the faint blush that warmed her cheeks at his scrutiny. Lifting her eyes as though she were concentrating on a particularly complex section of the music, she inhaled slowly, trying to calm herself. She was uncomfortable about being stared at so openly. It reminded her of her childhood, of the thoughtless remarks about her eyes. She wondered what Cotter was thinking now.

"Why garbage, professor?"

His unexpected choice of subject startled her. She gathered he was not a man predisposed to small talk. Somehow, though, the very directness of his query put her more at ease. She lowered her eyes to meet his, and smiled. "If you want to find out about a civilization, Mr. Hunt, just look at what's thrown away. Archaeologists study ancient garbage to learn about past civilizations. In this project, we'll be looking at today's refuse to learn about our cultural patterns."

There was a faint smile on his lips. "I suppose it would be hard to lie about one's garbage."

She laughed. "Exactly." Sitting forward, she added, "You'd be surprised about people—I mean, how they often say one thing and do another."

"Would I?" He arched one eyebrow. The expression wasn't particularly sincere, and though he gave no obvious indication of it, she was afraid he was making fun of her.

She sat back, resuming a businesslike manner. "I mean, in studies done in California, for example, only one family in four admits to drinking beer at home, but beer cans turn up in the refuse of three out of four households."

"Let me go on record, now, professor. I have been known to drink beer at home."

"Thanks, but we won't be examining your trash. Actually, choosing test locations is something I'll need your help with, though. We're hoping to compare two diverse socioeconomic groups: a low-income neighborhood and one that is basically wealthy."

"No problem. Unlike Robin Hood, I take from both the rich and the poor."

She was in the process of folding her hands in her lap when he made his little joke. She looked up, surprised by his wit. He wasn't smiling. She didn't know whether to or not. Opting for passively pleasant, she offered, "Good. If we could, Cotter, I'd like the neighborhood locations as soon as possible—by Monday, I hope. You see, we'll first need to interview residents in the specific areas. Meanwhile, this weekend, with your permission, I'll have the students get the stables set up as our lab."

He nodded. "You have my permission, but—" he looked skeptical "—don't people ever refuse to let you have their trash?"

"Well, I honestly don't know. This is my first time at this." She couldn't tell if he was really interested, but she decided she'd explain. "When we do the interviews, we assure everyone that privacy is ensured because we do our recording by census tracts rather than by directly identifying people. Only we know which house goes with which trash by a code number. No one else will. Why should they refuse?"

"On principle, I suppose."

She sat forward again, really interested. "Would you refuse a group of college students the chance to dig around in your trash?"

"Probably. But then, I take trash more seriously than do most people." He actually smiled, and his face changed entirely. Raine uttered a barely audible "Oh." He was a striking man. How ironic that she should notice his handsomeness when she was hardly ever any more aware of men than they were of her. Poor Cotter. He probably had a terrible time convincing women that he wasn't interested in them.

Raine decided that now was the time to tell him what she knew. She didn't care to analyze the reason she was so determined—so uncharacteristically compelled—to bring up the subject. She knew it would be awkward, at best. But somehow, she couldn't bear the idea of being a guest in this man's home and not acknowledging his lifestyle. This was the only way she could think of to express her sincerity and tolerance—letting him know that his preference didn't matter to her. She wondered how much companionship he really had, and the thought of him alone on the isolated estate made her sad. Bolstered by the thought that in the long run it would put their relationship on more honest turf, she ventured, "I—I think you are a man who values his privacy, perhaps more than most. Am I right?

His smile faded. He seemed to sense the tension in the air. Her heart went out to him. Right now her host's feelings were more important than her own, and she had to fight against her natural reserve. With determination, she moved toward him and placed a comforting hand on his leg. She was taken aback by how hard the muscles felt.

She faced him and looked directly into his dark eyes. They were wider than they had been a moment ago. Patting the leg reassuringly, she whispered, "I know all about you, Cotter, and I want you to know I respect your choice."

A wince dashed across his face before his expression changed to an incredulous frown. "You... understand."

It was an odd reaction, she thought. He didn't seem as amazed about her knowing that he was gay as he did about her acceptance of the fact. She nodded firmly, intent on convincing him that she meant what she said, "Yes, I do. Really." Removing her hand from his leg, she turned to address him directly. "I can't tell you how I know, only that I do. But, believe me, Cotter, I've been there, and I know how cruel people can be to those of us who are different. For as long as I can remember, people have hurt me the same way they've hurt you."

He regarded her warily. "You've...?" His eyes were penetrating as he looked at her quizzically. "Lord...you?"

She was nodding. "Yes. I know what it is to be treated badly, to be shunned and avoided, even laughed at."

He groaned, and she knew she'd hit a nerve. Putting her hand back on his leg, she added, "That's why I can say I understand, and that's why I'm going to tell you something that I've never told another soul."

He took her hand and held it tightly between both of his. There was pain in his eyes. "Look, professor. I don't want you to tell me anything."

"Oh, but I must—"

"No, you mustn't," he interrupted. "It's none of my business—"

"I'm making it your business." She put her free hand on the two that were crushing hers. She'd gone this far with it, and she couldn't back down now. "You've been so kind to allow us to stay here. I owe you this." She grasped his hands.

"You don't owe me this!" Releasing her hand he ran long fingers distractedly through his silver hair. "How could I have allowed myself to be talked into this?"

"Oh, please, Cotter, don't regret letting us come. I'm just telling you this to put us at ease." He opened his mouth to speak, but allowed her to continue. "You see, from my earliest memories, people teased me about being cross-eyed, and then, after the operation, when I got my glasses, I was still ridiculed." Without giving him a chance to say anything, she rushed on, wanting to get her distressing admission over with and finish as quickly as possible. "And I'm ashamed to admit it, but later, when I was put in special classes for the gifted, most of the kids I knew thought I was terribly strange, and they called me

The Brain. And even now I'm the old-maid schoolteacher." She felt her cheeks burn at the admission as she stumbled on, "So—so you see, I've spent a lot of time alone—like you..."

"Cross-eyed?" His frown melted into an expression of surprise. "You're talking about being called an old maid? That kind of different?"

"Yes. I felt that if you knew you weren't alone—that I've also had the experience of being avoided..."

With a shake of his head he repeated, "Avoided? Professor, I'd never have guessed."

"Well, I'd never have guessed you were gay." She bit down on her lower lip. She'd planned on being direct, but wondered if her approach was perhaps too explicit. Somehow all this hadn't seemed real until she'd actually said the word "gay."

After a long moment, Cotter responded with a chuckle. The sound was deep and rich. "So, you don't think I look gay?"

"No, not at all." Her eyes tentatively met his gaze. His open comment suddenly relieved her anxious tension. She'd expected this encounter to be much more difficult than it was turning out to be. Raine surrendered to a smile of embarrassment. Wanting to repay him for his show of character, she offered with honest enthusiasm, "Oh, it's quite true, Cotter. You're an extremely attractive man. It must be a challenge for you to convince women you aren't interested in them."

He ran a fist along his jaw, eyeing her closely. The black depths glitening. "You think so?"

"Uh-huh." She nodded ingenuously.

He stared at her for a long moment; then, with a wry grin, he took her hand in his, enveloping it in the warmth of his own. "I bet you took in all kinds of strays as a kid."

She lowered her eyes, admitting shyly, "I had to. I knew how they felt."

When he didn't say anything, she looked back at his face. He looked thoughtful for a moment before he glanced down at his watch. "I also bet you're hungry." He let go of her hand and stood up.

"I think I could eat...now," she admitted, feeling a great weight slide off her shoulders.

"Good." He held out his hand to help her up, and as she took it, he murmured, "You know, professor, I thought you'd take the information quite differently than you did. You surprise me."

She became inquisitive once again. "You knew I was aware?"

"I was informed." As he pulled her to her feet, he added, "You'll have to forgive my sister. She thought she was helping."

"Well, I don't understand quite how she thought she was helping," Raine admitted uneasily, "but now that it's all said and done, I'm glad. Aren't you?"

"Ecstatic." He nodded obligingly, but she could tell he was less than enthusiastic.

"No, really, Cotter. I think we could be friends if you'd give us a chance."

"You may be right. Few women have offered me their...friendship." His smile lacked humor. "And I bet having a garbage collector 'friend'—gay or not—is always good for a laugh at university functions."

She gazed curiously at his face for a moment. Highlighted by the lamp, his features were stark angles, his eyes indistinguishable in the shadowed depth below his arched brows, but there was a glitter in the darkness that she couldn't quite read. Pulling her gaze from his face, she scanned the bookshelves that spanned the wall to her right. Just at that moment, the album that had been playing softly behind their conversation ended and the room became so still that Raine could hear the call of a distant gull. Looking back up into Cotter's face, she wondered how it was possible that a man of his wealth and position could be intimidated by her education. But he was. Had she been wrong before? Could that be why he insisted on calling her professor instead of by her name?

Just when she was about to ask him why he had made such a ridiculous remark, he took her arm, and turned her toward the doors, suggesting mildly, "Let's go to dinner, professor. I'd like to meet the troops—especially the red-headed Lothario named Bill."

Bill? Her curiosity about this new, unexpected aspect of the man flew out of her mind like a canary escaping through an open window. "Why Bill, Cotter?" Her voice had taken on a slightly strained quality.

He halted, his hand on the doorknob. Looking down at her, he shook his head without smiling. "Don't worry, professor. My sister has a crush on him. My interest is purely in the role of concerned big brother."

She felt silly, and shrugged. "I'm sorry, Cotter. Of course you wouldn't—I mean, you'd never pursue an interest in my male students."

His lips lifted in a crooked smile. "Professor Webber, you have my word on that."

Turning toward him, she offered shyly, "Please, Cotter, call me Raine. I don't like titles."

He looked down at her and with a small nod, he agreed.

RAINE YAWNED AND STRETCHED. The warm water in the tub splashed and swirled about her as she rinsed the soap off her skin. The ride up, the stress of Nordie's revelation, the resulting talk with Cotter, the delicious dinner and now the tranquilizing bath—everything combined had made her exhausted. Leaning back against the warm marble, she thought about the dinner. It had been a lively meal, especially with Nordie's entertaining stories about rescuing a sailboat full of seasick Boy Scouts who had drifted into the waters near the Hunt estate.

She also recalled how Carl and Cotter had reacted to their vivacious sister. It was obvious to Raine that both brothers loved her dearly. Though Carl was pale and withdrawn during most of the meal, occasionally one of Nordie's outrageous remarks was enough to provoke a half smile from him. Raine felt sorry for the man, and she hoped that he would recover from his injury. Once a robust two-hundred-pound professional football player, he was now slumped in his wheelchair, pallid and thin, his dark eyes reflecting none of the fun in Nordie's eyes or the alertness in Cotter's.

She had been seated beside Carl at dinner and had tried to include him in the conversation, but usually his only response had been a vague nod. Before dinner was half over, he had excused himself and gone to his room. Nordie had been clearly upset by his departure, and Cotter had appeared less than happy as well. It was apparent that both of them were worried about him.

With a sigh, she stood up and reached for the plush towel that hung from a hook beside the tub. She patted herself dry before stepping out onto the marble steps that led to the carpeted floor.

Just as her foot sank into the deep pile, a door clicked open, and Raine froze, holding the towel draped loosely around her. Raine's gasp made Cotter stop in startled surprise. For a time that could not have been as long as it seemed, they stared at each other. Cotter was half naked himself and Raine's eyes were drawn to the white briefs that barely covered him.

He muttered something indistinguishable and backed out of the door he'd entered. It was on the other side of the large bathroom from the one that entered her own room. She'd noticed it, but had failed to check to make sure it was locked. She must have been more tired than she'd thought.

When the door clicked shut and Cotter was gone, she realized that she hadn't been breathing, and she exhaled deeply. Hurriedly, if belatedly, she wrapped the towel around her. Pulling the towel even tighter, she closed her eyes and counted to ten. Embarrassed and flustered, she felt a desperate need to regain her calm.

She jumped at the sound of a knock on the door, clutching tightly to the towel. "Yes, Cotter?" she replied, her voice faint.

"I'm sorry, Raine. I—I didn't know Nordie had given you Carl's old room."

"It's just fine." She gritted her teeth and continued, "it's forgotten." Even as she said it, she knew it wasn't and would never be. At least not by her. She could still see him looking so...male.

He mumbled a rather hoarse good-night and she nodded toward the door, not completely registering the fact that he couldn't know what she was doing. She felt listless, and she rested a hand on the edge of the vanity, wondering at the force of her reaction. Dropping the towel to the floor, she turned to look at her reflection. How flushed the warm water had made her—all the way up to her hairline.

She ran her hand across her cheek, gathering up loose strands of hair and smoothing them away from her face. She worked at logically reminding herself that Cotter would soon forget this disconcerting incident. After all, seeing her unclothed would mean little in the incident. After all, seeing her unclothed would mean little in the course of their relationship. Little? She amended the importance of the incident. Nothing, actually. It would mean nothing to him at all. Assuring herself of that fact should have eased her mind. But somehow, it didn't. And for a reason she couldn't fathom, she felt worse.

Chapter Three

"Surprise!"

Raine's fork clattered off her plate onto the tablecloth as she stared, stunned at the green creature that had just entered the dining room.

Nordie came to a clanking stop in a glamour-girl pose as tin cans, tied along the end of a fishnet cape, tumbled after her into the room. Raine's eyes widened at the outlandish costume. Besides having green skin, Nordie had on a bathing suit of the same color. Two grapefruit halves formed epaulets, and over her hips flowed a Hawaiian-style skirt made from a garbage bag cut in strips. On her feet she wore oversized wading boots, and her hair was tied in several places with grocery store twist-ties. She smiled broadly and graced her stunned audience with a curtsy. "Well, what do you think?" she asked smugly.

All conversation had stopped. Carl, who had been listlessly toying with his scrambled eggs, sat up a little straighter and stared. Cotter, who had been eating quietly across the table from Raine, set his coffee cup down. Resting his forearms on the table, he answered, "Since you ask, Nordie, I'm a little disturbed by the developments in the Middle East, but otherwise..." He let his words fade away with a shrug as he picked up his cup and took a sip as though it were common practice for her to appear at the door dressed like a shredded sack of garbage.

Raine switched her attention from Nordie's green face to Cotter's placid one. She'd avoided saying anything to him that morning, her memory of the embarrassing incident of last night still fresh in her mind. But under the circumstances, she couldn't help asking, "What's going on, Cotter?"

He raised unreadable eyes to meet hers. "Hmm?" He seemed not to know what she was talking about.

Nordie burst out laughing and plunked her hands on her hips. "Darn you, Cotter Hunt!" She clanked forward, her green brow furrowed in a mock frown.

"Not one foot closer, young lady." Cotter halted her in midstride with his words. "Don't get near this table. You'll contaminate the breakfast. What have you got all over your skin?"

She smiled then. "So, you did notice, after all."

He sat back, crossing his arms at his chest. "I noticed you've avoided resorting to sanity again."

Giggling, she grabbed the flowing cape and twirled on the Oriental rug. "This is sane, Cotter. Don't you know what today is?"

"I thought it was Saturday."

She clattered to a halt, laughing. "Besides that, silly. Today is the Dumpy Festival in Kennebunkport! I'm entering the Miss Dumpy contest. And I want you all to go and cheer me on."

Raine shifted her gaze from Carl, who had gone pale, back to Cotter. He didn't appear to be either pleased or displeased. It amazed her how his face could show absolutely no emotion. He suggested easily, "No one deserves the title more. But don't you have to be a resident?"

She waved off the idea. "I don't know. But I think I'll go and at least slip into the parade, I mean, as long as I'm dressed for it."

He arched a brow. "I think you ought to slip into an asylum."

She acted as though she hadn't heard him and hurried on, "Besides, with you being the biggest thing in garbage in this state, they ought to allow me special dispensation, don't you think?"

His dark eyes narrowed suspiciously. "I don't think you want to know what I think."

She sighed theatrically. "Oh, Cotter! Really." Then, spreading her arms in grand appeal, she asked the group at large, "What do you all say? How about a day at the festival? It's a quaint old town. We can eat at the old Perkins Mill and see the steeple bell cast by Paul Revere—maybe even see a play at the Garrick?"

The students began to talk all at once, their voices a deep-pitched rumble of enthusiasm. But Raine could hear Carl's negative murmur and turned in time to hear Cotter encourage Carl to make the trip. "It would do you good to get out."

"No." Carl's voice was nearly a whine. "I can't see being wheeled around. It's too much of a burden and I'm not up to it myself, either."

Raine pulled her lips together, feeling pained to witness this man's despair, but she couldn't tear her eyes from Cotter's solemn face. He leaned closer and whispered, "Look, Carl. Nordie's doing this for your sake. Are you going to break her heart?"

There was a pause, but Raine didn't turn away from Cotter to see how his words had affected Carl. She could only stare into his troubled eyes.

After a minute, Carl spoke just above a whisper. "I'm going upstairs now!" He backed himself away from the table with a single motion and wheeled quickly out of the room.

"Carl?" Nordie pivoted around to call after her brother, but he didn't stop and was soon gone. Turning back, she shot an apprehensive look toward Cotter, who only shook his head sadly.

Raine clasped her hands tightly in her lap as she watched Nordie absorb Carl's rejection. Nordie regained her composure and said, "Are we ready?"

The other students had begun to murmur enthusiastically, and Raine couldn't bring herself to impose work on them on a Saturday morning. She supposed they could get it all done tomorrow if they worked especially hard. So, instead of protesting, she replied, "It sounds like a unique experience, Nordie, but shouldn't you eat first?"

She shook her twist-tied curls. "Naw. Had grapefruit earlier." Unable to keep from responding to Nordie's antics, Raine smiled. She then turned, to see Cotter stand up. "Are you going, Cotter?"

He registered a slight surprise at the question before shaking his head. "I don't want to leave Carl here alone."

She stood as well. "Oh, why don't you go?" She knew he'd spend his time alone in some dark room. "You know, your advice to Carl is just as good for you. It would do you good to get out. I can stay here with Carl."

His look was startlingly direct. "And add another stray to your collection? No. You go and have a good time. Carl's not your problem."

"But you'd enjoy the festival and I could use the time to work."

"If you really want to stay and keep Carl company, Professor Webber," Nordie interjected hopefully, surprising Raine at her sudden nearness. "Cotter? Why don't you come with us. Professor Webber and Carl will be fine—alone." She emphasized the last word.

Cotter's smile disappeared. "Nordie, I'd like to have a word with you out in the hall, please."

"My slip showing?"

Cotter flicked his index finger at her as he headed for the dining room entrance, apparently expecting her to follow obediently.

Turning to Raine, Nordie whispered, "He likes to assert his authority in front of guests. You understand." Leaving Raine speechless, she clanked off hurriedly after her brother.

Cotter was standing with his legs braced wide and his arms folded across his chest when she caught up with him just outside the den door. "What is it?"

He addressed her firmly. "I'm not going to leave Raine and Carl here alone. You know I gave Hanna and Lys the day off."

Nordie jutted out her chin. "Of course I know all that. Good grief, Cot. It could be so perfect! They could get to know each other. But in order for them to do that, you can't be hanging around flexing muscles."

His tone was one of extreme exasperation. "Nordie, don't you understand...?" He let his words drop away. Of course she didn't understand. He hadn't told her the extent of Carl's injury and about his depression. Almost losing Carl had been a terrible blow to Cotter, bringing back the tragic loss of his parents with frightening clarity.

Changing the mood somewhat, he put a reassuring hand on Nordie's shoulder. "It's just that I have some work to do."

"Oh. Well..." she said, relenting, "I guess it'll be okay." Raising a warning finger, she added, "If you stay out of sight and leave them alone."

He snorted derisively. "I'll try."

"You'll try, huh?" She eyed him suspiciously. "I suppose that'll have to do. It is your house."

"Sometimes I wonder." He gave her a casual jab. "Now, get out of here."

"Okay, okay. Don't get physical."

Raine and the young men had begun to filter into the entry when Cotter and Nordie reached them. "Well, guys—" Nordie nodded good-bye to Raine as she took Bill's arm and guided him toward the door "—we'd better get ourselves on down to the festival before they run out of beer."

Raine called after her, "Do you have a change of clothes?"

"Sure." Nordie flashed a sparkling smile through green lips. "Nordie Hunt is always prepared—like the proverbial Girl Scout."

"The color's right, anyway," Cotter interjected mildly.

Without missing a step, Nordie waved at him over her shoulder. "I'll ignore that. I know how cranky you can be when I get the last grapefruit."

RAINE SAT LISTLESSLY in the deck chair, watching the ocean, and tugged absently at the scooped neckline of her bathing suit. She didn't swim often or well, and bathing suits seemed to her a poor substitute for real clothes—not quite appropriate for public exposure.

In the past hour she'd counted seventy-three sea gulls, and she couldn't remember the number of waves that had washed up onto the sparkling white sand. Her eyelids had grown heavy, and she had to work at staying awake. She didn't know why she was working so hard at something that didn't really matter. Carl had been sitting by the pool when she'd come out. But he'd stayed for only fifteen minutes, while she'd struggled to make conversation. Then he mumbled that he was going to his room. To be truthful, she was relieved when he left. Poor Carl. She sighed out loud. But it wasn't Carl she was thinking of now. It was Cotter. She hadn't seen him since breakfast, and she pictured him brooding in his den.

"Well..." she said to herself aloud, "if I sit here much longer, I'll only get depressed myself." She swung her legs off the chair and took one final tug at the suit as she headed down the steps toward the beach. She pushed her glasses up on her nose and squinted at the blue sky and strong sunlight.

Accustomed to solitary walks, Raine felt exhilarated at the prospect of exploring the strip of beach ahead. From where she stood, it looked as though the beach narrowed to almost nothing at the point. She felt sure that on the other side there was a secluded stretch, and she liked the idea of seclusion; if she did decide to sunbathe in the skimpy suit, she would be sure of her privacy. One thing she didn't plan on was swimming. She'd never been in the ocean, and she certainly didn't intend to go in now unless there was someone else around who could keep a watchful eye over her. It looked to her like a big place in which to drown.

The closer she got to the cliff, the surer she was that she'd been right about the place. The only problem was that she would have to wade out about knee-deep into a rough area where the sea broke against the rocks. But across the obstacle, around the bend, she could see a wide patch of beach. With a measure of resolve, she straightened her glasses and set out through the shallow water.

"Oooff!" she groaned as something hit her in the stomach with such force that she lost her footing and toppled backward into the water. She inhaled as her head went under, and salty brine washed over her. Flailing wildly, she coughed and spluttered, unable to get a breath.

She felt strong arms lift her from the water and instinctively grabbed for her rescuer. Her eyes burned. Looking up into the bright sun made it worse, so she shielded her eyes behind a warm, wet shoulder.

As her body was gently lowered onto the sand, her rescuer uttered reassuring words. "You'll be okay in a minute."

She took in a gulp of air, registering that the voice was oddly familiar. Her eyes flew open to see Cotter's blurred face close to her own. As he released her, he sat back and looked at her, his expression closed in concern. "Professor, I'm sorry. I didn't see you there. Here—" he held out a blurry hand "—I rescued your glasses."

"Oh, thanks," she whispered hoarsely, slipping the glasses on with shaky hands before gingerly touching the bruised skin of her stomach. "What did you hit me with?"

He shook his head in self-disgust and motioned toward the water where a full garbage bag was sinking slowly below the rough surface. "Trash." He leaned forward. "I was cleaning up the beach. The easiest way to get the bags across the rocks is to toss 'em. I didn't see you coming." He saw her hand resting protectively over the thin fabric of her suit. "You're not cut, are you? There was some broken glass in there."

She looked down at the black nylon. "No—no." She leaned back on both elbows, inhaling deeply. Her throat felt raw, but at least now she could breathe again. Still feeling slightly dazed, she watched him through narrowed eyes. "I guess I'll live."

The glint of unease that flickered in the depths of his eyes disappeared. "I'm glad." He sat down on the sand beside her, and Raine noticed for the first time that he was wearing a pair of khaki shorts, now soaked and clinging to his hips and thighs. He wore no shirt, and seawater glistened on the dark mat of hair that covered his chest. He certainly looked all man—broad shoulders, long legs, deep tan. With an effort she shook off the errant thought, pulling her eyes back to his face. He was not smiling, and she noticed with interest that he seemed lost in thought, as if something else were occupying his attention.

When she realized what, she hurriedly, sat up, self-consciously tugging at the suit to recover her modesty.

"Here, Raine," his fingers closed around her wrist, and she found herself being pulled to stand. "Let me help you up. Do you think you can walk now?"

She was steadier than she had thought she would be. "Yes...of course." She looked out to where the bag had been floating. Just the top was visible as it crashed against an outcropping of rock. She nodded toward it. "Maybe you'd better get that before it gets torn up and makes a mess."

He nodded, and with several long strides, he reached the bag and dragged it onto the beach, dropping it beside two others. When he looked at her again, she shook her head at him, smiling tentatively.

"What's funny?"

"You're taking a busman's holiday—coming out here on a Saturday picking up trash."

"Carl was so depressed, I gave him something so he could sleep." He ran a hand through his hair, ruffling it. "It's frustrating not to be able to do more. Physical activity helps me take my mind off...everything."

Her heart went out to him. Without thinking, she touched his hand. "Do you want to talk about it, Cotter?"

His sad smile was appreciative as he shook his head. Taking her elbow lightly, he suggested, "Why don't we walk." Turning her away from the point, he asked casually, "Do you have a boyfriend, professor?"

The question took her by surprise. "Me? No." She could have told him about Jerry, her "almost." He'd pursued her for a couple of years when she'd been a graduate student at the University of Arizona, but somehow, her work had always seemed to come first. And eventually, Jerry lost interest, concluding that Raine wasn't ready for a relationship. And that had been pretty much how it had gone ever since; her work interested her more than any man she'd met.

For some reason, she just hadn't felt...whatever it was that she was supposed to feel. In the past few years she'd decided that the element needed to make a woman fall in love just hadn't been given to her. Maybe her abundant intellect had something to do with it—She used her studies and, later, her work, as a convenient excuse not to get involved and not to risk feeling strong emotions for a man.

Hoping that the oppressively long pause hadn't been too revealing, she cast a furtive glance toward his profile. "I'm not involved with anyone right now," she said. Now it was Raine who seemed distracted, and Cotter realized he'd touched on a sensitive area.

He changed the subject abruptly. "How about a swim?" He halted, turning to face her.

With difficulty, she met his eyes. "I—I don't swim well, and I've never been in the ocean."

"Then you ought to try it."

She looked into his eyes and felt the tension of the moment before drain away. "I suppose...if you promise there aren't any sharks."

His smile was fleeting but amiable. "I promise."

She shook her head, an involuntary smile forming on her lips. "Do you lie much?"

He frowned slightly, feeling lousy about the elaborate deception. "Only when cornered," he admitted. Trying to shake off his feeling of guilt, he added wryly, "But I never lie about sharks." Lifting her glasses from her nose, he laid them on a rock before taking her hand. "Come on," he coaxed.

She followed him reluctantly, until the water was swirling around her shoulders. "Cotter?" she queried.

"Yes?" He inclined his head toward her, feeling a tug of compassion when he saw the fear in her eyes. He imagined the ocean could seem overwhelming to a child, but he was touched by Raine's genuine sense of awe at the ocean. It struck Cotter as a metaphor for her awe at everything outside the protected world of academia. She didn't often venture outside the university—he would have to remember that.

"How much farther are we—" She felt a sharp pain. "Cotter! I think something's bitten me!"

Cotter's arms came around her automatically. He held her securely to him, sure that she was reacting more to fear than anything else. To reassure her, he began, "Raine, I doubt..."

"It got me just above the ankle." She reeled, pressing herself against him.

He tried a lighter approach. "It couldn't have been a shark. I would have seen—"

"Then it was a jellyfish or an eel!" she cried weakly. "It hurts."

Completely baffled, but becoming alarmed, he held her tightly and lifted her from the water. She clung to him, feeling vulnerable, but trusting him to examine the wound. "Raine—" the exertion made him a little breathless "—we're out of the water, but I don't think..." He looked down and saw the source of her discomfort. Several spines had lodged in her ankle, and the skin around the punctures was irritated and beginning to swell. "Sea urchins—nothing to worry too much about. Bear with me while I take the spikes out; you'll be fine in a minute."

He deftly removed them while Raine did her best not to flinch. When he was through she felt compelled to explain—in fact, to rationalize—her fear. "Excuse me, Cotter. I'm just so unused to the water." She looked up embarrassed.

When their gazes met, the contact was complete. "Everybody's afraid of something." He was looking at her, but he was imagining quite another setting, far removed from the present circumstances. "With me, it's fire." The words came out just above a whisper.

She searched his dark eyes, wondering where he'd gone. Once again she became very aware of how strong his presence was and found herself feeling terribly drawn to him as his empathetic response comforted her. An urge to return his confidence—to pay him back for his kindness—overwhelmed her. "You know what's really strange?" she asked softly.

Her question brought him instantly back, his eyes alert but guarded. "What's that?"

She winced, biting down hard on her lip. She'd taken him away from his private thoughts now and began to wonder about whether or not to continue.

Cotter's face closed. "Mind if we sit? I'm a little weary."

Feeling weak herself, Raine joined him on the sand.

He bent one leg and curled an elbow around it. The movement brought them so close that she could feel the radiant heat of his arm near her shoulder. Almost in a whisper, he said, "You don't have to explain anything to me, Raine."

"I know, but it's important to me that you understand how I feel, Cotter. I'm comfortable with you." She considered her words. "I've never felt this way with a man before." She paused briefly, as his face registered distress. "Oh." She pressed her hand on his forearm. "You're a caring person, Cotter. You're easy to talk to. I'm glad we're here, together. Tell me," she coaxed with a shy smile, "aren't you surprised at how things are working out between us?"

He watched her for a long, troubled moment before he took her hand into his. She was too sincere a person to lie to, and he hated himself for having been manipulated by Nordie. In an unhappy tone he muttered, "Yes, very surprised." At least that was true.

She felt reassured by his reply. "Good." On an impulse that came out of nowhere, she kissed his lean cheek. "Friends, then?"

His brows dipped. He'd never had a woman "friend" before. Lovers, yes, plenty of them. But female friends? Never. He didn't even know any men he could really call friends. That was the way he'd wanted it, though.

He didn't want intimacy in his life, didn't even want friends, because that was the first step toward intimacy. Years of feeling guilty about his inability to save his parents had made him see very clearly the danger of intimate relationships. He was responsible for Carl and Nordie. His cowardice had deprived them of their parents. He'd sworn years ago that he'd never let anything happen to his siblings again, and he'd done his best since then. They were his brother and sister, and he loved them. But he didn't need or want anyone else. He had enough responsibility—all the family he wanted.

Raine had put her glasses back on and was looking up at him with trusting eyes. He lied to her, would go on lying to her, yet she had no inkling of it. He wondered if she'd still want his friendship if she knew. He ran a hand through his hair, looking away.

"Cotter?" She touched his arm and he turned back. She looked so wistful, this shy, intellectual professor. He felt uneasy in the pit of his stomach. He could be pretty hard-boiled when it came to women, but something about her innocent request elicited his protective instincts. Or maybe the ludicrous plan of Nordie's was getting to him.

With all the untruths he'd told her, maybe he owed her something—even if it was just extreme politeness. Besides, it was only four weeks. What could it hurt to humor her? What was one more lie if it made her feel better? Not very proud of himself, he nodded. "All right, professor. Friends."

"Raine," she said with a smile. Her buoyancy and the relief that glowed in her eyes made her features blossom. Sitting back, she relaxed visibly. He had the uncomfortable feeling that even that was a form of trust, of belief that she had found a friend, and he winced inwardly.

"Cotter?" She sighed, squinting up at the sky. "Do you suppose Nordie will win the title of Miss Dumpy?" she mused aloud.

He grunted, a bitter smile twisting his lips. "As far as I'm concerned, she already has."

Chapter Four

"Well, I'm totally disenchanted!"

Raine's eyes shot up from the charts that she had been studying when Nordie flounced into Cotter's den. When she saw that it was Raine sitting behind the desk instead of her brother, she stopped short. "Oh, Miss Webber. Pardon me. I thought—"

Raine smiled up at the pixie-faced girl. "Cotter had some helpful information run off for me concerning the socioeconomic areas that Scavenger Hunt's service covers. I was just going over it, choosing possible study areas."

"Oh?" Her polite show of interest amused Raine. "Say, where are my wayward brothers, anyway? The guys and I got in so late last night I didn't see them. And I was busy getting the stables cleaned and set up, so I haven't seen them all day."

Raine adjusted her glasses and tried to remember. "Well, I think Carl is in his room. And Cotter went in to Portland for the afternoon, I believe."

Nordie nodded. "I guess I'll catch them at dinner. What are we going to be doing in those stables on all those long tables Lys has been setting up?"

Raine searched for accurate words to describe the classification process. "Well, twice a week, big plastic bags from selected areas will be delivered. We'll open them and painstakingly examine, classify, weigh and record everything we find."

"Everything?" Nordie cried theatrically.

Raine nodded, smiling. "Every scrap. Our trash bears the very imprint of our life-styles." She imitated Nordie's dramatic gesture.

Her student laughed. "It's a pretty powerful imprint—if you go by smell!" She shook her head.

"We'll be methodical and serious about this, Nordie," Raine admonished, but there was a smile in her voice.

"Oh, I'll be serious, Professor Webber. Tomorrow." She grinned. "Meanwhile, we're all going swimming. Sort of wash away the stable dust. You want to come?"

Raine swallowed uneasily. "In the ocean?"

"Uh-huh." Nordie giggled. "I'm going to have Bill teach me to swim."

Raine was surprised. "Really? I would have thought you could swim quite well, living so near the ocean."

"I can. But there are a couple of strokes I can still learn—from Bill." Her expression was coy.

"Oh, I see." Raine rested her chin on her hands, wondering at the girl's maneuverings. Such playfulness would never occur to her. But who could judge her tactics? Raine certainly had no relationship to use as an example. "Well, good luck." There was a slight sigh in her words.

"Thanks. See you later, Professor Webber."

"Nordie?" Raine was curious.

She brushed a curl out of her eyes as she turned back. "Hm?"

"Did you win the Miss Dumpy contest?"

"No, and that's why I'm totally disenchanted!" She tossed her head with disdain. "Some bank president's daughter won! She wore a disgusting necklace of fishheads and, well, actually, the whole outfit was so disgusting I can't bring myself to talk about it."

Raine wrinkled her nose. "It must have been awful, if you are too fainthearted to describe it."

"It was! I mean, I had no idea that anyone would go to such extremes of bad taste. But—" she nodded her head with determination "—next year, I'll be prepared!"

Raine sat back. "The mind boggles."

"Don't it just." Turning away again, Nordie exited with a flourish. "'Bye for now."

With a wry grin, Raine returned to her chore of selecting two sample neighborhoods. She went back to the computer printout of Cotter's recommended areas and made a notation on her pad. Time passed, and before she realized it, Hanna was knocking on the study door. "Miss Webber? Dinner is ready. Will you come, or shall I serve you in here?"

Raine sat back and stretched. She'd just made her final choices, right on schedule. "I'll come, Hanna. Thanks." Gathering up the pages and her notes, she stuck them into her briefcase and headed toward her room. "Hanna," she called after the cook, "I'd like to take care of a couple of things. Do I have a few minutes?"

The gray-haired woman turned back and smiled sweetly. "Yes, ma'am. Miss Hunt is gathering up her boys. So I imagine it will take her a little time."

DINNER'S MAIN DISH, a magnificent lamb shoulder with spinach stuffing, had just been served when Hanna entered with a message. "Mr. Cotter, you have a guest in the living room."

"Correction—dining room," a measured voice interjected as a tall woman in a sleek white silk dress appeared behind Hanna. Her hair was straight, black and thick, and skimmed her bare shoulders. Wispy bangs shadowed large, slanted eyes of sparkling onyx. Raine could only describe the beautiful stranger as svelte. A model, perhaps? She tried to guess at the glamorous woman's career.

Raine turned to Nordie in time to see her startled gaze. Nordie's reaction made it plain that the woman's appearance was a surprise to her. "Anona!" she breathed. "What are you doing here?"

The lovely woman swept past Nordie, laughing. "Hi, Nordie. Start any world wars while I was away?" She shook her beautiful hair and smiled down at the girl. "Actually, I got through in New York earlier than I'd expected, and I just had to get back." She scanned the room full of students. "Well, well. I seem to have crashed a party." With hardly a pause, her eyes fastened on Cotter, and she added, even more softly, "Hello, darling—" she beamed at him "—miss me?"

Cotter leaned back in his chair and shifted a narrow look across the table toward his sister before lifting an engaging smile toward Anona. "Of course." He pushed his chair back from the table and stood up, reaching out to take her hand as she floated toward him. "Won't you join us?"

"I'd love to, Cot—"

"Oh, that's wonderful! Naturally, we've all missed you, beyond words!" Nordie bounced up from her chair and clasped her hands together in glee that was just short of hysterical. "Uh, everybody, this is Anona Witlong, uh, Dr. Witlong—our, uh, family psychiatrist."

Anona tilted her head around and peered at Nordie as Cotter burst into a hearty fit of coughing.

Nordie bounced around the table, waving her napkin. "Oh, Anona, there's something I've been dying to tell you but knew I'd have to do it in person. It just can't wait another minute." She grasped the taller woman's arm and steered her toward the door.

"But I came—" She was prevented from saying anything else, because Nordie had already escorted her from the dining room.

Bill was first to speak. "You're family's got its own psychiatrist?"

Cotter appeared to be battling a grin. "Don't you think we need one?"

Bill's quizzical expression eased into a wide smile. "I don't know about that, but Dr. Witlong doesn't look like any therapist I've ever seen."

Cotter put a hand on the back of his chair and situated it so that he could take his seat again. "Have you seen many?"

Bill laughed and shook his head. "No. But that's obviously been my loss."

"Spend much more time with my sister, and I'm sure you'll get your chance." Nodding towards Hanna, who was visibly confused, Cotter directed quietly, "Please set a place for...the...for Anona, Hanna."

"Yes—yes, sir." She backed into the door that led into the pantry in a stupor, and Raine wondered what was wrong with the woman. Ordinarily, she seemed imperturbable.

"Why don't we eat? I'm sure the ladies will be back shortly," Cotter said as he took his seat, and Raine's eyes were once again drawn to him. There was something inexplicable about his manner; he was so much more knowing than he let on. His choice of words indicated that he retained complete control— he never seemed to be flustered, only amused by his sister's eccentricity. "Raine?" Cotter's voice interrupted her train of thought, and she blinked up to meet his dark gaze.

"Yes?" Her cheeks felt warm, and she hoped that she wasn't blushing.

"I just asked if those printouts I gave you are what you need."

"Oh." She nodded a bit disjointedly. "Everything. As a matter of fact, I'm glad you brought that up." She turned toward her students. "We'll need to have a meeting right after dinner, and I'll outline our plan of action for tomorrow." Turning back to Cotter, she asked, "Where would we be out of your way?"

"You won't be in the way, professor, but," he suggested casually, "I suppose the den would be most comfortable."

She nodded, but lost her chance to answer as Nordie and the doctor reentered the room. Nordie was pointing out each student and naming him in turn. "And finally, Dr. Witlong, this is our instructor, Professor Raine Webber."

"I'm happy to meet all of you." Anona seemed somewhat ill at ease. "Nordie has explained everything—" she switched her gaze to Cotter "—about the project. It sounds...unique, to say the least. I wish you all luck."

"Thank you." Raine could think of nothing else to say. But it was just as well, because Nordie had drawn Anona's attention away with a whispered phrase.

Hanna bustled in with a bundle of silverware and immediately busied herself beside Raine.

"No!" All eyes were drawn to Nordie's stricken face. She blanched and smiled sheepishly. "I—uh—Hanna, I'd rather we save that place for Carl, just in case he decides to join us. Why don't you put Anona on the far end. Next to Cotter." With a wordless nod, Hanna scooped everything up and scurried around the table.

When she had gone and the women were seated, Nordie asked, "So, Professor Webber, how did you do on your own yesterday? All work and no play? I certainly hope you didn't do anything I wouldn't approve of." Her grin was devilish.

"I shudder to think what you wouldn't approve of," Cotter quipped.

Raine's smile was shy. "Actually, Nordie, Carl spent most of the day in his room asleep. I didn't do much work, and Cotter and I took a walk on the beach."

"You did?" Two voices in unison asked the same question. At least it was a question on the part of Dr. Witlong. From Nordie, it sounded like an accusation.

Raine looked from Nordie to Anona and then turned toward Cotter, who had just cleared his throat. He was in the process of cutting a bite of asparagus, his eyes on his plate.

Raine nodded to no one in particular, confused at the degree of interest. She decided to address the doctor's question. She was certainly aware of Cotter's alternate life-style. Hoping that her remark would be cryptic enough to pass over the heads of the students, Raine offered helpfully, "He was most entertaining company."

Nordie responded cattily, "He must not have been himself."

Anona patted her lips with her napkin. "Oh, I don't know, Nordie. Cotter can be quite... entertaining."

"Thank you, doctor." Cotter's eyes swung lazily to meet her gaze. "Will there be a charge for that?"

Her slanted eyes narrowed slightly with the broadening of her smile. "Count on it."

Cotter's eyes sparkled as he took a sip of his iced tea, but he said nothing.

"Doctor," Bill offered, "Do you have any patients like Sybil?"

Anona replied cautiously, "Sybil who?"

"Sybil," Cotter helped. "You know, doctor, one of the most famous cases of multiple personalities ever recorded."

"Yes." Bill leaned forward, his elbows on the table. "She exhibited sixteen separate personalities. Do you have similar cases?"

"Oh, *that* Sybil." Anona's smile dimmed noticeably, her eyes scanning the expectant faces around the table before she turned pointedly toward her host. "Cotter—"

"No kiddin'!" Bill exclaimed. "You mean, it? Mr. Hunt has multiple personalities?"

"Oh, no, I didn't mean that Cotter has sixteen different personalities."

"There are eight million weirdos in the naked Cotter!" Nordie chimed in, mimicking a deep announcer's voice.

A guttural sound came from Cotter.

"Kidding! Just kidding!" Nordie answered, shrugging broadly. "Anona? Why don't you answer Bill's question, and I'll keep my mouth shut."

"Actually," Anona offered quietly, "I don't have any patients like that. Sybil's case was a rare—and exaggerated—one. In fact, your question reminds me of something I need to communicate to your host." She turned slightly in her chair and covered Cotter's hand with hers. "Alone. Do you mind?"

Raine wondered at the practiced poise of the other woman. Cotter, too, was relaxed and cordial, even seeming somewhat interested. Raine watched, transfixed, as his well-formed lips lifted in a smile. "Would you care for dessert first?"

"Later." Tilting her dark head, Anona granted him an unusually flirtatious smile for a doctor.

He gave her a brief nod before turning to the rest of the company. "Will you please excuse us."

"Good-bye, Nordie, Professor Webber, everyone," Anona intoned sweetly as she took Cotter's arm.

There were echoes of the statement around the table. Raine lowered her gaze to her plate, feeling strangely unhappy. If she didn't know better, she could swear that she was jealous of Anona, drifting like a white mist out the door with Cotter. She shook her head, distressed with her response.

She closed her eyes and tried to think of nothing—nothing at all. But she couldn't get the vision of Cotter's silver head bent obligingly toward Anona as they walked away. She crumpled her napkin nervously. Maybe it wouldn't hurt her to have a session with the doctor, too!

THE LAST OF THE STUDENTS drifted out of Raine's meeting. She got up from Cotter's leather chair and walked to the tall windows to look out at the grassy slope that led down to the beach. A full moon illuminated the point of land where she'd run into Cotter the day before. Above the rocky area, on the cliff, a glimmer of light caught the undulations of the tree branches, set in motion by the ocean breeze.

The den was dark now, and quiet. She hoped that her students would use their better judgment and go to sleep early. Five o'clock in the morning would seem impossible, otherwise. But they had to be at Cotter's company headquarters by six-thirty in order to go with the trucks as they made their pickups. They would begin doing interviews and gather up and tag their first samples.

She stifled a yawn. It must be close to ten-thirty—time for her to start thinking about getting to bed, too. Raine decided on a brief walk before retiring. Impulsively, she headed out of the room, striding past the entry hall, past the columns of the porch and down the steps. As she was about to turn into the garden path, a flash of white fluttered into view on the cliff. Raine stopped, squinting curiously. The ghostly figure grew larger, stepping from behind a tree, out toward the edge of the cliff. There was no mistaking the lovely white silk dress. It was Dr. Witlong. As Raine watched, another, taller figure appeared from behind a crop of trees. The light color of his shirt and slacks, and the silver glint of hair, identified the man.

Raine considered the couple and wondered faintly why Dr. Witlong was spending so much time with Cotter. Surely her current interest in the Hunt family would be Carl. His depression was so evident that even she, untrained in the area of mental health, knew that he needed help. Perhaps the doctor was discussing Carl's condition with Cotter before she saw him, to get a better understanding of Carl's progress—or lack of it—during her absence.

Suddenly Raine's expression froze in a stare of disbelief. The doctor had turned away from the ocean, lifted her arms to Cotter's neck and raised her face to his. And now they were locked in an intimate embrace, kissing.

Kissing? Raine's wide eyes were riveted on the entwined couple on the cliff. Anona's flowing white dress seemed to be caressing and enfolding Cotter as they embraced. What was going on? Raine swallowed, realizing that her throat had gone dry as she watched the couple, openmouthed.

Her mind couldn't grasp what she saw, unable to get a firm hold on why a female psychiatrist was kissing a male patient who was supposedly uninterested in that sort of thing. Before she realized it, Raine was walking briskly, a crisp breeze teasing her short hair, as she hurried along a path of crushed clam shells winding through a garden—toward the point. Stumbling to a halt, she pushed her glasses more securely on her nose. For the first time, she became acutely conscious that something was very wrong. And something very basic inside her wanted answers—sound, clinical answers. She had to admit that she didn't know what kind of therapy was currently considered successful with patients like Cotter, but somehow, she didn't feel comfortable with Anona's methods. Almost involuntarily, Raine continued her approach.

"Darling." Raine stopped abruptly when she heard Anona's throaty endearment. Barely breathing, she listened as the doctor went on. "Why can't we go back to the house? I haven't seen you in two weeks. Surely your professor friend and her charges are asleep by now."

Raine strained to hear Cotter's murmur. "I think it would be better if you went home, Anona. It's bad enough that we're out here together."

Anona groaned. It was a sensuous sound. "But Cotter, what's the point of this whole crazy stunt, telling that mousy professor that you're gay so she'll keep her hands off you? I know you're irresistible, but isn't that going overboard?" she mused. "I cut short my buying trip for the store because I wanted to be with you, and you're telling me to go home? I ought to go back to New York and leave you to act out the part. It would serve you right."

"That might be best, Anona," he whispered. "I told you before, it can't be helped."

"Oh, darling, it isn't fair. For once, would you think of us, and forget Carl and Nordie and all their crazy problems?"

The ensuing silence told Raine that the two were once again clasped in an embrace. She strained to piece together their words. Mousy professor? Act out the part? What exactly had Anona said? "Telling that mousy professor that you're gay so she'd keep her hands off...." Raine pressed a burning cheek to the rough bark and closed her eyes. Anona Witlong was no doctor. And Cotter Hunt was definitely not gay. That much was clear. But could any man possibly be so conceited that he felt he had to ward off "mousy" professors with wild stories about sexual inconsistencies—and what was worse, enlist the help of his little sister and his girlfriend in doing so?

Raine knew she was no femme fatale. But she had no idea that any man would go to such lengths to avoid her! She licked a tear from her lip. The next one she wiped away angrily with a trembling hand, almost knocking her glasses off.

She turned away and leaned weakly against the tree trunk. She knotted her hands together as the full effect of Cotter's prank took hold. How he must have laughed at her naive belief in his story. And he surely must have gotten a kick out of her admissions about herself told to him when she'd thought he'd understood the pain of being different. She could see him shaking his head at her professorial account of what it was like to be shunned.

Dropping her head, Raine tried to control her sense of betrayal. Now she knew the real reason he'd been amused so much of the time. He could afford to be polite—the joke was on her. And she knew why, on the beach, he'd been so remote. His whole objective had been to stay away from her. She thought she'd understood his unease. How wrong and foolish she'd been!

Her lips began to quiver, and she hugged herself to restrain the trembling. It was odd that she felt so devastated to find out that Cotter Hunt had no problem with women—he just didn't want to cope with her! Usually, it didn't make much difference to Raine how men felt about her. But Cotter's ploy really hurt. How could she have allowed herself to be duped by a man with such an enormous ego? And how could she have been so wrong about him? She'd even told the man she liked him and insisted on his friendship! Good Lord! He must have squirmed at that.

She blinked away tears and stared up at the moon. "Damn!" she cursed in a soft whisper. *Well, my dear Mr. Hunt,* she vowed silently, *no need to worry about my amorous attacks. I'll keep my hands off you with pleasure!*

Tugging at the skirt of her shirtwaist, she tried to focus on the house. It was especially blurry from this distance. Making her steps as soundless as possible, she headed away from the cliff, from Cotter and from his unforgivable deception.

But another thought gnawed at Raine, and she struggled to repress it. More than anything, she wanted to run to her car and escape to her apartment at Orono. But the anthropology project loomed before her; it was too important to drop just because she'd been hurt and humiliated. After all, the students were depending on course credit, and she was counting on the money. Personal feelings would have to be shelved and controlled. She'd managed that way all her life. She would just have to manage again.

When she reached the path to the garden, she decided to walk off her frustrations. Wandering among the bushes and ornamental shrubs seemed like a good way to heal her wounded spirit. The air in the garden was filled with the scent of damp earth and roses. She breathed deeply, trying hard to recapture her objectivity, and walked farther into the tangle of foliage.

An old-fashioned bench appeared in the darkness, and Raine sat down. This place certainly was secluded. Perfect for her state of mind. She had just seated herself and leaned back against the cool wood slats when she heard voices in the distance. She couldn't make out the words but, from the tone, she could tell it was an argument. She sat straight, listening. Cotter's deep voice was not raised, merely coaxing. But Anona's was shrill. After a brief, final outburst, Raine heard the thud of a car door and then the roar of a motor as a car squealed past.

Raine frowned, listening. The stillness was so complete that it was intimidating. She could swear that Cotter had not gone with Anona, and it was clear that he was not following in his own car. She didn't know if she could hear the front door close from here. Probably not. Cotter, no doubt, had gone inside.

She sat back again, wondering if Anona had decided to go back to New York. It seemed so. And as Anona had said, it would serve Cotter right. The gravelly sound of footsteps on the path made her stiffen, and she looked up in time to see a tall figure approach. Realizing it was Cotter, she bolted to her feet.

When he saw her, he stopped. His face was barely visible in the shrouded darkness, but Raine could see a glint in his eyes as he scanned her from head to toe. "Well, hello." White teeth appeared in an easy smile. "I had no idea anyone was still awake. What are you doing out here?"

How dare he act so...so innocent. She blinked back hot tears as her anger surfaced. Her emotions were clouding her reason, though she tried to see the situation clearly. With a bitter smile quivering at the corners of her lips, she lifted a trembling hand and pushed him aside, heading for the house.

He recovered his footing and was about to speak when Raine interrupted, grinding out fiercely. "Oh, don't panic, Cotter. I'll keep my hands off you! You're not nearly as irresistible as you think!"

Whirling away, she ran down the path, aware only of the hot sting in her eyes and the odd, shadowed look in his gaze.

Chapter Five

Cotter pulled his Land-Rover into the cavernous garage. In his side-view mirror he saw his sister, clad in a white lab coat, pink rubber gloves, jeans and sandals. She was running toward him, waving something in the air. Shaking his head, dreading the consequences of her enthusiasm, he stepped from behind the wheel and closed the door. He leaned against the car door and waited for the evening's bizarre greeting.

"Cot! Cot! Get a whiff of this." She was short of breath by the time she'd run all the way from the converted stables. She waved a limp, green-black object under his nose. The stench was unnerving. He clasped her by the wrist and lowered the object from his face. "Why the hell are you attacking me with a rotten pickle?"

She beamed at him. The past week of working on the study had made Nordie happy. That made one of them, anyway. She was laughing. "How did you know it was a rotten pickle?"

He ran a hand through his hair, smiling faintly. "Do you forget? Our roots are buried deep in rotten pickles. Wait until you run across a diaper—or spoiled chicken. Now those are smells worth writing home about." He dropped a hand to her shoulder. "But don't share the experience with me. I've smelled it all."

She clutched the pickle behind her back. "Oh, yeah. Our fortune is built on a foundation of refuse."

"Well put." He cocked his head in the direction of the stables. "Don't you have something important to do with that pickle—preferably far away?"

"Naw." She turned away and dropped it into a covered trash container. Peeling off her gloves, she added, "It's been logged. We don't keep the garbage; we just record it."

"That's a relief." He put his arm around her shoulders. "You about finished for the day?"

"Completely." She patted his hand. "Maybe you'd better not touch the coat. I'm not sterile."

"I'll take my chances."

They strolled in silence up the front steps. At the door, Nordie turned to face Cotter. "Say, did you know a cop was out here today? Talked to Professor Webber for a while. Something about an investigation of some guy we're collecting garbage from.

We're supposed to check his garbage carefully for some reason."

Cotter lifted a brow. "Hmm. Do you know why?"

She shook her head. "Professor Webber probably does. She's going to take the guy's garbage personally. The cop—Detective Nooner, or Neuter, something like that—said the garbage study was a real stroke of luck for them. Wouldn't arouse suspicion, with us collecting everybody's trash on that street."

They resumed their walk as Nordie chattered on. "You can ask Professor Webber the details. I just think it'd be exciting if we helped put some criminal behind bars."

He laughed. "Nordie Hunt, public servant—private pain in the neck."

She poked him in the ribs. "Thanks a lot!"

With a grunt he let go of her. "I'm going to do a little more work in my study tonight. Would you mind telling Hanna to bring me my dinner in there?"

Nordie wrinkled her nose in irritation. "Again? Every night this week?" She narrowed her eyes suspiciously. "What's so important in the trash business lately? I realize that with you absent, Professor Webber has been paying fantastic attention to Carl, but you don't have to put yourself into solitary confinement for him. Besides, I miss you when you're not around."

Her genuine expression melted him completely, and he beckoned to her. "Come into the study with me for a minute."

Once they were inside and seated on the couch, he watched her face, enjoying the quiet moment.

"Well?" She slipped off her sandals and curled her feet beneath her. "What's up?"

"The jig, little Miss Fixit."

She scratched her ear, eyeing him curiously. "What's that mean?"

"It means, Professor Webber knows I'm not gay."

She gasped, clutching his hand. "You don't mean it! How? You didn't tell her, did you?"

"No." He shrugged. "She either saw me with Anona, or heard something last Sunday night." He leaned his head back and stared up at the ceiling, recalling the hurt and anger in her face when she pushed him. "She told me I'm not exactly irresistible."

There was silence for a moment, when all he could hear was the rhythmic ticking of the grandfather clock in the corner of the room, and his thoughts mulled over the past five days. He'd wanted to say something to Raine—something to let her know that the pretense wasn't just the cruel prank of a boastful playboy, as she apparently thought. But every time they had come face to face, in the hall or a room, she had either quickened her step or turned and headed in the opposite direction.

The last time he'd seen her had been that morning. They'd happened to come out of their rooms at the same time. As soon as she saw him she spun around and retreated into her room. He waited for a moment, wanting to knock at her door, wanting to tell her about Carl's dangerously depressed condition, about Nordie's practical jokes. The pain and hurt magnified in her huge, soft eyes bothered him more than he cared to admit. But he couldn't betray Nordie or Carl. Besides, the sensitive, young professor had turned her nurturing attentions toward his ailing brother. He knew that. He'd seen Raine and Carl talking several times. Perhaps what had happened had been for the best in the long run. Still, somehow, Cotter felt a very real sense of loss every time she turned away from him.

He was drawn from his sober reverie when Nordie burst out in a delighted laugh that sounded uncomfortably like the cackle of a lunatic hyena. "Oh! She called you on that one!" She was wiping tears of laughter from her eyes.

He lowered his gaze to her. "Your sympathy warms me all over. Did I mention she pushed me? That should make your day."

"Pushed you?" She shook her head, giggling.

He sat back, frowning. "Do you find everybody's pain funny, or just mine?"

She took his wrists, pulling his hands into her lap. Pressing her lips together, she tried to calm herself.

"Don't you see the beauty of it, Cotter? Here I was working so hard at getting her not to notice you by telling her that you were gay—when the truth is what actually did it. You are full of yourself, *Mr. Irresistible.*"

He balled a fist and touched her chin with it.

She took the fist in both of her hands. "Okay, okay. I know you're no egomaniac. But what difference does it make? We're getting the results we wanted, aren't we? How were we to know how she'd react? You figure her out."

"I have enough trouble figuring *you* out."

Nordie seemed not to hear. "Did Professor Webber shove Anona, too?" Nordie shook her head, giggling. "Now there's a conceited something—and *uninformed*. Anona couldn't tell Joyce Brothers and Anna Freud apart if her life depended on it. Imagine her asking, 'Sybil who?' I almost choked on my food."

"Impossible. You haven't choked on any of your words. But no, she didn't push Anona. Anona left before Raine and I...talked. Anona went back to New York, I guess." Cotter walked to the window and looked out. "Anona has her good qualities; she's just a little spoiled." He paused for emphasis. "Speaking of spoiled, if *you* feel like going anywhere, don't let me stop you."

"Okay, I get the hint. But before I go, I think you should know something. There's an invitation for a big charity bash at the Penells'. It's tomorrow night. Luckily, I found it under a pile of junk mail. Weren't you intending to RSVP?"

He turned back, frowning down at the desk. The silver-lined envelope lay torn open in full view, with the engraved invitation standing beside it like a tent. Impossible to miss. "I planned to send them a check. You know I hate those kinds of affairs."

"I know," she agreed more gently than he'd expected. "But you're going." She raised her arms inclusively. "We all are. I accepted for us."

He shot her a sharp look. "You did what?"

She nodded, her mouth set in a determined line. "It won't do you any good to rant and rave, Cotter. It's done, and everybody is looking forward to it. Even Carl. And besides, with an intelligent woman like Professor Webber as our houseguest, I figure it might help your image. Some of those tunnel-visioned snobs might quit looking down on my entrepreneurial garbageman brother." She folded her arms across her chest, nodding in thought. "Oh, I realize that she isn't your type—you like 'em shallow and dumb. But do the Penells of the world have to know that? I mean, for once let 'em see you with a real lady on your arm."

"You're unbelievable," he mumbled tiredly as he dropped into his chair. "The woman doesn't want my arm. She wants my head."

Nordie didn't seem to have heard him. She was checking her watch. "Well, I'd better get showered before dinner. See ya."

Cotter remained quiet as she scooped up her sandals and left the room. Rubbing his temples, he focused on the invitation, feeling a headache coming on.

FOR ONCE IN HER LIFE, Raine was running late. But before scurrying down the curved staircase to the formal living room, she tugged again at the ruffled straps that kept slipping off her shoulders. She cursed in frustration. She'd never worn a dress quite so opulent or revealing. The wide scoop of the neck did more than hint at cleavage, and she wasn't used to explicit clothing. With one last, calm-gathering breath she started down the stairs. The spiked, champagne-colored heels forced her to hold on to the railing. Even though she was moving down the curved staircase very slowly, the silk chiffon dress fluttered and billowed around her legs. She paused, touching the off-white dress. It was covered with hand-cut eyelash squares of glittering gold Lurex, making the cloth seem like gossamer. It surprised her a little that Nordie would lend her such an extravagant party dress.

With a nervous swipe at her hair, she entered the aqua-and-beige living room, decorated with French

Provincial furniture. There was a rustle and a scraping of chairs as the men stood.

"Wow!"

Raine turned in the direction of the sound and smiled at George, a bookish student who rarely spoke unless spoken to. He was blushing uncontrollably.

"Thank you, George. You look very nice, too." She felt her own cheeks redden but tried valiantly to keep her poise. With an effort, she raised her chin a bit higher and scanned the large room. "All of you look wonderful. I've never seen you so dressed up before." Movement from the far corner of the room caught her eye, and she turned. To her horror, she saw Cotter walking toward her. His smile was courtly and his presence disturbingly regal. The perfectly groomed head of hair shone in the light of the chandeliers. His white dinner jacket flattered his broad shoulders. A black bow tie and gold cuff links provided elegant accents.

She lowered her eyes but continued to watch his graceful, broad stride. She had to admit, despite her disappointment in him, that he was a very attractive man. But—she reminded herself sternly as he took her hand—he very well knew it!

"You look lovely, Raine."

In her mind she scoffed at his compliment. The remark was merely a social requirement, but it had its effect. Working to keep her voice even, she admitted, "The dress is Nordie's. I didn't bring anything appropriate for a formal party."

His lips opened in a surprised, "Oh? Well, for once, my sister came through." He turned to look at her and smiled. "I've never seen this dress, Nordie."

She hugged Bill's arm and giggled. "I bought it in a fit of conservatism after the last presidential address. Never could bring myself to wear it, though."

"I doubt that the president was referring to conservatism in party attire, Nordie, but for you, it would be a start," Cotter quipped, as he scanned his sister's day-glo suit and matching pumps. He shook his head.

She laughed again, squeezing Bill's arm. "I knew you'd be pleased."

During the exchange, Cotter had continued to hold Raine's hand, and it had been a strain for her to follow the conversation. When he gently squeezed her fingers, she realized that he was speaking to her, and her eyes shot up to meet his. "What?"

He repeated, "I asked if you'd like a drink before we go."

She swallowed. "I...no. I've kept everybody waiting long enough."

"All right, then, I've sent for Lys to take Carl out the back way, down the ramp, so I believe we're ready to leave." He moved a hand to her back, guiding her toward the front door. She could feel his fingers spread as his hand rested there possessively.

On the trip over, Raine was quiet, trying to concentrate on Nordie's chatter. But it was hard to think straight with Cotter so close at hand. Carl was on her right, making the small luxury car seem very full. Nordie, Bill and George occupied the backseat. Their caravan of two cars wound slowly along the coast road toward Portland and the Penells' estate, near Bramhall's Hill.

Her thoughts drifted from Nordie's humorous anecdotes. What was Cotter doing, treating her as if she were his date? She had gone along with it in front of her students, but she certainly didn't intend to allow him to get away with his ploy, whatever it was. She planned to make it very clear to him that he was not irresistible in any sense of the word. She grimaced, shifting away from his touch. Looking down at her hands, she curled them tightly in her lap. Of course, acting the gentleman was more familiar to him than acting like a gay man, but neither act portrayed him as his true self.

Later, when the party had been going on for some time, Raine found herself in the same cluster of guests with Cotter. In the maze of well-dressed, wealthy people, the conversations had been inconsequential, boring or unbearably smug. She was stifling a yawn when she realized that Cotter was there. As she was about to leave, a fragment of the conversation caught her attention. A tall, distinguished-looking man was speaking a bit too loudly. He sloshed a glass of whisky in Cotter's direction. "Say, old man, are you following this, or would you like me to explain?"

Raine's eyes widened in disbelief at the man's condescending remark. The sneer of superiority was evident, and she shifted worried eyes toward Cotter, who was leaning against a marble hearth. To Raine's surprise, he smiled pleasantly back at the man. "I believe I'm following you, Josh. But at a respectable distance, of course." Straightening, he nodded toward the group, but his dark eyes found hers and held them an instant longer than necessary. "If you'll excuse me?"

Raine watched him walk away. She'd seen him retreat many times that week. He hadn't known that when she brushed by him, more often than not she'd turn back and watch him; she didn't know why. And after a week of watching him walk into the distance, she felt that she was a pretty fair authority on how he looked. This time there was something wrong. To the others she was sure he appeared calm and cool, but to her, his gait seemed less confident, not quite as assured.

A lump rose in her throat. Of course. The man was hurt. Cotter Hunt—wealthy, handsome, intelligent, the manager of a prosperous and vital business—was hurt by what this person had said. For some reason, Cotter felt inferior to these people. She was stunned to realize it, but he did understand how it felt to be looked down on, to be snubbed—but in a way she could never have guessed.

Turning back to face Josh, she lifted her chin, ready to fight for the underdog. She cleared her throat, halting murmured conversation in the small group, as all eyes turned to her. "Perhaps if you had a fraction of Mr. Hunt's intelligence and acumen, you'd be a little more gracious toward him. Are you following me, old man, or would you like me to explain?"

She pivoted away as the other men burst out laughing. One of them clapped Josh on the back and guffawed loud enough for her to hear. "Say, Josh, the lady sure nailed you with that one. I'll have to remember that remark the next time you give me bum advice on the market."

When her anger receded, Raine felt awful, and for ten minutes she took refuge in the master suite's powder room. How could she have insulted one of the guests like that, and in defence of a man she couldn't stand? She hated the idea of returning to the party. But she couldn't stay in the bathroom all evening. Rallying, she peeked out into the bedroom. A fluttering of sheer curtains drew her gaze to a balcony. She could hear raucous laughter filtering through the open doors and realized that the balcony must lead around to the main living room. Maybe, she thought, she could bear the evening by spending time on the balcony.

Breathing deeply the cool moist air, she stepped out under the stars. Distant lightning flashed, serving as a fiery backdrop to the majestic mountains far off in New Hampshire. Raine smiled despite her mood. Somehow the eloquence of nature could always make her feel at peace—especially when she was beset by man-made problems.

"Raine Webber, champion of the underdog." The voice was so soft it seemed to fit right into the velvety night. Still, Raine's knuckles tightened their grip on the iron railing as she turned toward the sound of Cotter's voice. He was very still, standing partly hidden by a pillar. When she turned, he stepped out from behind it and walked to her side. Supporting himself on the railing, he looked off into the distance. "Why did you defend me in there?"

Her lips parted in surprise. "How did you..." The words trailed away as he turned back, his face so close, so masculinely beautiful, that she lost the ability to speak.

His whisper feathered her upturned lips. "It spread through the party like wildfire."

She looked away toward the mountains. Cotter's lips, so near her own, were unsettling. She tried to keep her mind on the subject at hand, whispering harshly, "The man is an insensitive fool. I've known too many people like that in my life to let him get away with that remark." She added defensively, "What I said was a knee-jerk reaction."

"Nothing personal, then." The words sounded vaguely wistful, and Raine turned back to face him. For an instant his facade slipped and she could see the lonely man inside the shell. His dark, brooding eyes held hers as he added quietly, "So I may assume you still detest me?"

She'd meant to be stern with him, aloof and cool, but her resolve broke down when she confronted him. Her heart went out to him and she offered truthfully, "I—I don't detest you, Cotter, not really. But I feel badly bruised; it was just so unnecessary."

She could have sworn, for an instant, that relief shone in the dark depths of his eyes. But too soon it was gone, his eyes narrowing to slits as his sensuous mouth curved down. He stared at her for a long time, his mood edgy. "Damn it!" he began with a growl, startling her. "Why don't you hate me? You should. I wouldn't blame you if you did."

She felt the sudden touch of his hard lips on hers, and his arms pulled her against him as he muttered, "Hate me" against her lips. She was stunned, confused by his abrupt action, and opened her mouth slightly to question. But before she could speak, she received a kiss that was pulsating and deep. One of his hands moved up her back and began a firm, tingling massage at the nape of her neck. The rough, exciting sensations he was creating in her sent conflicting messages to her brain that she couldn't decipher and didn't want to. Something that wasn't

Raine Webber, the shy, intellectual professor, sparked to life and took control of her gestures.

Her fingers spread, her hands searching along his broad back. He was so responsive, yet so solid, and the pounding of his heart tingled against the palm of her hand. Her lips quivered as she inhaled his musky scent, which mingled pleasantly with faint cologne, the damp air and the soft aroma of wild sweetbrier.

His lips became more pliant, nipping at hers, and his tongue played along her teeth, moving with excruciating deliberation to explore the sensitive skin behind her lips. His kiss deepened farther, and some part of her, a part that she never guessed existed, opened itself fully to the sensuality of the moment.

He traced her cheek with gentle kisses, until he was caressing the back of her neck with his lips with a tenderness she hadn't known in him. Her head lolled back as he began to be conscious of what he had allowed to happen.

With arms trembling to keep from crushing her to him, he groaned, pulling himself away. "Raine," he pleaded, "go inside. I...this is no good." He tensed, reaching for her. Fingers tightening on her arms, he bit out angrily, "I don't want to be one of your strays. I don't want your friendship. I just want to be left alone."

Her lips parted slightly and she uttered an expression of pain. At her strangled cry, he dropped his arms as though her skin had burned him. Stumbling away, she backed into the cold iron railing and curled her shaky fingers around it to keep from taking him back into her arms. No man had ever affected her so deeply before. Every instinct in her demanded his touch. It had happened so quickly, almost as quickly as he had ended it. She swallowed, blinking up at him in confusion, mindful of his rejection while her body quaked.

He dropped his head, running a hand through his hair and leaning against the railing as though he, too, needed support. *"Damn."* He shook his head and looked up at the sky. "Don't look at me that way."

Pressing trembling lips together, she turned away and adjusted her glasses. Unable to restrain herself, she rasped out shakily, "Why did you kiss me? Just to prove you could?"

His sigh was audible. "I don't know."

She laughed bitterly. "The truth? I didn't think it was in you."

"Raine." He moved to face her. His features were tense. "I know that story about my being gay seems like a dirty trick to you. But I can't explain why I lied."

"Can't or won't?" she challenged.

"Okay, won't," he confessed with an unapologetic lift of one brow.

A breeze ruffled her hair, blowing it across her face. With an irritated motion she pressed it behind her ear. "Thanks. That makes it easy. Detesting you will be my pleasure from now on."

"Damn it, Raine!" His fingers tangled in her hair so that he could turn her face up, forcing her eyes to meet his. He suddenly wanted her gentleness back, wanted her liquescent eyes to smile at him again. Going against all he'd ever thought he wanted, he avowed, "That's not really what I meant. I—"

"Well, it's what I meant!" With an angry shake of her head, she pulled away from his touch. "I'm going inside to find Carl. It's getting unpleasant out here."

A crack of thunder masked his gritted curse as the first cold drops of the approaching storm spiked Raine's cheeks and bare shoulders. Once inside, she was relieved that no one could distinguish the raindrops from the tears that glistened on her face.

Chapter Six

"Why aren't you getting ready to go clamming?"

Raine dropped the catsup bottle onto the plywood table and spun around at Cotter's surprise visit to the empty stables.

"Oh," she breathed, stunned by his appearance. "You startled me." Trying to seem distant, she leaned back on the heavy plywood surface, nodding in the direction of the beach. "Actually, I didn't figure I'd be much help. I don't know how."

He continued to walk toward her. "And you don't care to learn." It wasn't a question. Though he didn't smile, she could tell his remark was a veiled reminder of her aversion to the sea. Feeling disconcerted by the flash of memory, she turned away, recapturing the bottle she'd been about to catalogue. "I—I'm not finished. I've got to do this batch." She picked up a marking pencil and wrote down the appropriate code on a recording sheet for the computerized data bank.

She felt his nearness and knew that he was leaning over her shoulder before he spoke. "What are you doing?"

Soundlessly she cleared her throat, moving slightly away from him as she reached for the next item. "You wouldn't be interested."

"Yes, I would."

She frowned. Was he edging closer? She couldn't be sure.

"Don't you have trouble writing with those gloves on? Here." Without waiting for her answer, he picked up a pencil. "Just tell me what to write."

She recalled her former resolve. She was going to be civil, that was all. "Well," she admitted, "we do usually work in two-man teams."

"Then consider me your man," he murmured quietly.

She stiffened at the words and the way they were said. His day must really have been boring for him to go to such lengths to get a rise out of her. She ignored him, pulling a hunk of overdone roast beef from the plastic garbage bag. "Okay. Start writing." She put the meat on a small scale. "Put 203 grams in the column marked 'waste.'" She pointed to a laminated legal-size piece of paper filled with columns of code explanations. "Look on that for the code number for beef and enter that."

Raine kept every scrap of conversation between them strictly business as she pulled one thing and then another from the garbage bag. "034, cracker—one item, brand Sun Meadow, type saltines, composition E."

He looked up from his writing. "E?"

"It's a plastic wrapper. 'E' stands for plastic. Remember, earlier we had a composition 'F'? That was paper."

He nodded, entering the letter "E" in the appropriate column.

"Hmm." She pulled out a scrap of paper. "I wonder..." She was staring at the sales receipt with some figures scribbled on the back when Cotter's question interrupted her thoughts.

"What do you wonder? It's an 'F,' isn't it?"

She shook her head, almost smiling. Certainly he must wonder what her hesitation was. They'd already had several grocery sales receipts that had caused her no hesitation. She decided to explain. "Yes, it's an 'F.' Go ahead and record it. But I was just wondering if this might be something that Detective Noonan could have meant."

"Detective Noonan?" Cotter recorded the letter and laid the pencil down. "Is he the policeman Nordie told me about, the one who came out here last week?"

Raine nodded, deciding to keep the slip of paper. "Yes." She bent down beneath the table and dropped the paper into a small metal box. "He asked me to save everything—any notes, figures, phone numbers, even doodles." She pushed her glasses up on her nose with the back of her wrist, not wanting to look directly at Cotter. It had been four days since the party—since the kiss—four days since she'd even spoken to him. Since then, their paths hadn't crossed. He'd been at his office in Portland until quite late every evening. That was until today. Unluckily, it looked as though he was going to be at home all day, because it was just past noon.

"What's this guy done?"

She pulled a beer can from the bag. She examined it with undue care, not wanting to look at him. "He's reputed to be some sort of powerful crime boss, I guess. Detective Noonan says they're trying to get evidence on him for any one of several felonies—drug trafficking, loan-sharking, pimping and extortion." She fingered the can in her hand, "095, beer can—one item—"

He broke in. "I don't know, Raine. This sounds pretty dangerous to me. I'm not sure it's a good idea for you and the kids to be involved."

She looked up at him, surprised. "Why?"

"Why?" He looked down into her wide eyes. "Extortion? My God! What if this man found out his trash is being checked by the police—and that a naive lady professor is helping. What do you think they'd do, come over and ask you nicely to stop? I thought you knew better than that."

She stiffened at his remark. "Well—well, first, the kids aren't involved. I'm doing this all on my own. And about its being dangerous, I consulted Detective Noonan on that. He said as long as the whole block is being monitored, they wouldn't get suspicious. He said even if this Ed Fusco did get curious enough to check with the university, he'd find that the project had been funded six months ago—long before the investigation began—plus, since Nordie is involved in the project, it would be only natural for us to use your service. Detective Noonan said the whole project would be considered just a coincidence." She looked away from his probing, doubtful eyes, lowering her gaze to obscure all but the can from her view. "I'm satisfied. I can't help it if you're not. Brand, Old Country Dark, composition—"

"I just hope you're right," he interrupted her mechanical recital. "And I damn well hope Dectective Noonan is one hell of a cop, too. I don't relish the idea of my sister and a bunch of innocent kids being mixed up with gangland bosses."

Raine swallowed, attempting to go on, but she felt an unreasonable stab of pain when she wasn't included in his concerns. "Uh, composition 'R.'"

"Composition 'R.'" He mumbled it like a curse as he wrote it down.

She pulled out a plastic cup. "056—"

"And you, for God's sake!" He slammed down the pencil. "You're a babe in the woods if I've ever seen one. Anybody—a hit man, for that matter—could walk up to you on the street, feed you some sob story, and you'd rush off with him—probably get yourself wasted in the bargain. Lord, Raine, whatever you do, don't go wandering around Portland alone while you're involved in this. And for heaven's sake, don't tell anyone what you're doing!"

"You really do think I'm a fool, don't you!" She slammed the cup down as vehemently as he'd slammed down the pencil. "Well, you ought to know! Reigning king of sob stories! But, don't despair, you've taught me a great lesson. Believe me! I'll think twice before I'm taken in by a sad story again. I hope your influence on me has made you very happy!"

He stared at her in stony silence, his jaw working furiously. Then, after a long moment, he turned away from the table. "Hell, I didn't mean for us to get into an argument when I came out here." He turned back to face her, placing a hand on her shoulder. "Just be careful, will you?" He lowered his gaze to the table, his features drawn, almost sad. "What did you say the code is for the paper cup, anyway?"

She felt her throat constrict slightly, a reaction to his unexpected softening, and she nervously shifted her eyes to the smashed cup. For a moment, her mind fumbled with code numbers. And then all she could see in her mind's eye were his long, warm fingers resting near her skin and the half-smiling—almost caring—look he had just passed over her. She stuttered, "Uh—the c-code?"

He lowered his hand and picked up the pencil. "Never mind. I remember. 056. Right?"

She couldn't be sure if he'd said "056" or *"2001: A Space Odyssey."* Nevertheless, she nodded. It was all she could think of to do.

RAINE WAS ENJOYING her leisure time on the beach, under the pretext of digging for clams. "Uh-oh," she said, sighing, as she spied a small hole and a tiny spurt of water that told her a clam had detected her approach and pulled in its head. "*Go away!*" she whispered, sidestepping the spot and heading in the opposite direction, a clam bucket sloshing half full of clean seawater in one hand and a flat-tined clam digger in the other. She had no intention of facing any more creatures of the deep, dinner or no dinner. Even so, she'd sat patiently through Nordie's detailed lecture on everything she ever wanted to know about digging clams. She breathed a sigh of relief when she learned that hot dogs would also be served; at least she wouldn't starve.

"Hey, you've missed three since I've been watching. What are you thinking about?"

Raine spun around, the right leg of her slacks drooping back to her ankle from its rolled-up position. "I—I." She shrugged, giving up on trying to make up a story. Cotter was standing there, a well-dressed clam digger in a black-and-white-striped pullover knit shirt and black corduroy shorts. He, too, was carrying a bucket and digger. She wondered if he'd been more diligent in his efforts than she. Of course, anyone not unconscious would have been more diligent than she. She simply wasn't trying at all. Shrugging, she dropped her digger and bucket with a muted "clunk" in the wet sand. "I've decided to have hot dogs for dinner."

Cotter laughed. "I thought so. You're afraid of clams, too."

Even though she knew he'd see the truth in her strained face, she bent over to roll up her slacks and lied, "I'm not afraid of clams. I just don't like the taste of them."

"Really?" He didn't sound convinced. "What do they taste like?"

She swallowed, her cheeks warming. She had no idea what they tasted like. But it wouldn't do to let him know that. She felt panic rush up her spine, but she decided to try to bluff, anyway. "Come now." She straightened, eyeing him suspiciously. "Haven't you ever tried clams?"

"Sure."

She secured her glasses against her nose. "Then you ought to know what they taste like. Why ask me?"

His smile was exceedingly slow to bloom, beginning with a twitch at the corners of his mouth and then curving upward to reveal his straight, even teeth. His smile was as dazzling as white sand at noon—and curiously friendly. He walked toward her with athletic grace, and as he reached her side, he put down his bucket, already half full of soaking clams, she noted with displeasure. He nodded toward their feet. "See there?"

She saw the tiny spurt he meant but pretended not to. "Uh-huh, your feet are bigger than mine. So what?"

"Maybe if you took off your glasses..."

"If I took off my glasses, I couldn't even be sure if we had feet," she retorted testily, squinting back up at his face. He was still slanting that smile at her. She wished he'd relent; her tolerance was beginning to wane.

"You're being a coward again, professor. The sea and its creatures are not that deadly. Here—" he handed her his clam digger "—try it." The wooden handle was shoved into her hand, and she clasped it tightly. "Holding on is a good start." He put his hand on her shoulder and pointed in front of her right foot. "Dig there."

She stared at the spot as though it were a dead fly.

"Dig."

With a sigh, she dropped to her knees and pressed the prongs into the sand. A few energetic thrusts fueled by tension and a fear of the unknown pulled her shelled treasure to the surface, hitting her on the thigh. A scream welled up in her throat but she stifled most of it. "I didn't know they attacked!" she said tentatively, her thumb and forefinger poised a safe twelve inches above it.

"They rarely do. Now pick it up and put it in the bucket."

She cast him a pinched look. "Rarely?"

His chuckle was deep and rich. "If it wounds you in any way, I promise, you'll end up in the *Guinness Book of World Records* as the first victim of a clam attack."

His exceeding good humor irritated her. She looked down at the clam and, with a resolve of steel, clamped it between her fingers and flung it madly toward her bucket.

"You missed," Cotter reported the obvious as the clam rolled two feet on the other side of the bucket.

"Oh, shut up." She scrambled to her feet and scurried after it. This time, she deposited it deliberately into the water. One clam. "Well..." She wiped her hands together. "That's that. I'm going back."

"Back?" He picked up his bucket. "There's no reason to go back that way. Nordie and her crew have it pretty well covered. We might as well head on down around the point."

"We?" She started at the word, quickly making an excuse. "I don't intend to go through that again."

He shook his head incredulously. "For a woman who has her hands in garbage all day, I'm surprised you're so squeamish about clams."

He had a point, but it wasn't the important one. The real issue was that she was squeamish about Cotter. He'd been giving her double messages since the beginning. And for the life of her she couldn't understand why he was there. She decided to try another tack. "I think I'll find Carl and help him dig clams."

The slight lift of Cotter's chin, as though it had been clipped by a small fist, told Raine that he'd gotten the message. "Carl had an appointment with his doctor this afternoon. He's still in Portland. He'll be back for the clambake, though. I'm sure he'd appreciate it if you dug him some clams." Cotter's dark gaze drifted slowly away, toward the point. "So would Nordie."

"I gather you would, too, since you're out here pressuring me to dig them."

He shrugged easily. "I didn't figure you cared what mattered to me. But, yes."

"You're right. I don't care." She looked down. A squirt caught her eye and she knelt. "Okay, then. Here's one for Carl." She forked the sand away and extracted another clam. This time she felt an unexpected exhilaration with the successful find as she tossed it into her bucket. "That's two."

"Don't you really like the taste of steamed clams dipped in melted butter?"

"Never tasted 'em." She was not watching Cotter now; her eyes were glued to any movement in the sand. When she heard him chuckle, she directed a stern look at him. "What's so funny?"

He lowered his bucket to the sand and took her by the elbow, drawing her into a slow stride. "Did I catch the professor in a lie?"

She pulled out of his grasp. "Okay, I lied. But, I don't think that exactly makes us even—if that's what you're trying to suggest." A bubble of water caught her eye, and she dipped to one knee and began clawing at the wet sand with abandon, her nerves on edge.

When she had tossed number three into her bucket, Cotter took her arm again, helping her to her feet. "You don't have to maul the poor things, you know."

"You don't have to stay here and watch." She pushed away a strand of hair in a familiar gesture and looked up at him. "You getting squeamish, now?"

"Touché." He nodded, dropping to his knees and digging up one clam and then another in practically the same hole.

"Two! How did you know?"

He tossed one of them into her bucket, and one into his, before standing up. "I could hear her passionate moaning."

His unexpectedly suggestive remark shocked Raine into silence, and she could only stare up at his half smile.

"You have a very attractive blush, professor," he murmured barely above a whisper, as he stepped closer. "That's a rare thing these days."

She took a step away, protesting, "I wish I didn't—"

"Don't say that," he whispered, touching her cheek. "It's nice."

His hand felt damp and sandy against her skin. She couldn't draw away, even when he ran his fingers back through her hair. "It's also nice how you fight your timidity," he murmured softly, tucking a finger beneath her chin. "I like that about you."

She dropped her eyes, feeling embarrassed and uncomfortable, unused to male flattery. She needed to escape, but she also needed to be in his presence a while longer.

"Hey," he breathed against her ear, "it's the truth."

She stiffened at the word that had become a call to battle between them. But he was ready for her resistance, pulling her possessively against his chest, his lips taking hers quickly and solemnly. After the first kiss, his movements changed, becoming more incessant, warming, vitalizing her to her core. Her cheek felt hot against his, and the cool roughness of his jaw was a pleasing texture.

His lips moved pliantly against hers, draining them of all stiffness, all reserve. Her mouth sought the intimacy he was offering as her arms caressed his broad back. She sighed against his lips. It was a soft, purring sound that she could not have imagined coming from her throat. It seemed almost exactly like the sensuous, feminine moan that Anona had breathed the night Raine had seen them on the cliff, wrapped in each other's arms....

Anona! Raine's eyes flew open with the memory. Beautiful, sexy Anona, entwined in Cotter's arms. With a painful rush, it all came back to her, his unbounded conceit and unexplained deceptions.

What in the world was she doing, allowing him to kiss her? She pulled her lips into a tight line and stepped back quickly. It was harder than she imagined it would be, and anger raced through her like fire in a parched forest. Pulling away completely, she pushed him away from her.

He pulled her back, but she was prepared to flee. The look he leveled at her was enigmatic. She swooped down to grasp her bucket handle, and set off, jogging, in the direction of the point.

"Raine," he called after her.

She didn't turn or hesitate, but followed the shoreline at a quickened pace.

Her arm aching from the weight of the clam bucket, Raine trudged back along the beach. Swiftly, she rounded the rocky point, surprised at her almost casual leap across the watery obstacle. The tide was coming in, and as she jumped across, the waves splashed up nearly to her hips. But the sea didn't frighten her anymore. She'd gotten the knees and the seat of her sky-blue slacks so caked with sand that now the ocean water didn't matter.

Her nose was sunburned and tender where her glasses rested. Even so, her mood was fairly light, considering everything. She had to admit that digging for clams had become fun—like hunting for treasure and finding it. All in all, in the hour or so since she'd left Cotter, she'd had a good time. She looked across the beach, up toward the house. The setting sun had become a magenta backdrop, making the house appear dark in silhouette. Only a few lights glowed golden from inside tall, first-floor windows.

She heard the sound of youthful laughter, and turned back toward the sandy stretch ahead of her, her eyes drawn to a roaring bonfire with shadowed figures milling around it.

"Professor Webber! Professor Webber!" She heard Nordie calling long before she could make out her slender figure. The girl was clad in a white terry robe, and her curly hair was wet and glistening in the fire's glow. "We were about to send out a search party. You okay?"

Raine smiled tiredly as two of the students rushed up to unburden her, taking her bucket and digger.

She sighed with relief, thanking them. "I'm fine. Just pooped."

"No kidding. You've got quite a batch, there." Nordie motioned to a row of deck chairs that had been brought down to the beach. "Grab a seat and a glass of cider or some white wine while the guys get these babies ready for the steam kettle."

A long table was set up behind the chairs. It held plates, glasses and a variety of utensils. There was a gallon bottle of sweet apple cider at one end. Underneath the table was a tub filled with ice where several bottles of white wine and more jugs of cider cooled. Raine scanned the scene, looking for Carl. But when she located him, sitting quietly, staring blankly into the fire, she did not immediately walk over to sit beside him. Her eyes continued to wander among the moving human shapes in the flickering darkness. A little surprised, she realized she was looking for Cotter.

"Wine?" Anona Witlong stepped into her view with a stemmed glass and pressed it into Raine's hand. Her smile was bright and beautiful. "Cotter thought you'd like some." Without pausing, she went on, in conversational patter, "I offered to bring it to you. I wanted to speak to you alone for a minute. And apologize for that little joke the other night." She shifted uncomfortably, and Raine noticed her fashionably short, kimono-style beach robe. "It's just that some members of the Hunt family are incurable pranksters. I hope you'll forgive me. But, you understand, there wasn't much else I could do."

Trying to hide her surprise at finding Anona there, Raine wet her lips with the wine, pretending a nonchalance she didn't feel. Then, with a small, unreproachful shake of her head, she assured Anona, "Don't worry. I don't blame you."

Anona's eyes sparkled. "Thanks. You're being a good sport, I must say. Of course, you know I'm no psychiatrist. I have a store in Portland—sell lingerie. It's called Lace and Things. I hope you'll drop by before you leave. I give a ten percent discount to friends. Oh, Cotter." She extended an arm and Raine followed the movement of the long, slender fingers until a larger, familiar hand took the mauve fingertips in a light grasp. "Darling, I was just telling Raine about my place downtown." She turned back to Raine. "Anyway, Raine, I'm glad the truth is out. I'd just about given up hope of seeing Cotter until after the project was over—then this afternoon, out of the blue, he calls and tells me you know everything, and invites me to dinner." She laughed. "I tell you, that Nordie—"

"Yes, Nordie is motioning to us," Cotter interrupted, putting a firm hand at Raine's elbow. "I think she wants you to know your batch is going on to steam." As he spoke, he steered both women closer to the fire. "If we were going to go all out, we'd have dug a hole, filled the bottom with hot rocks, covered them with wet seaweed and then put the clams on top in wire-bottomed boxes. Then, we'd have covered the whole thing with a tarp. But that's really best for big groups—a hundred or so people. We usually put a couple of big kettles on the fire, fill the bottom half with seaweed, and dump the clams on top. It's easier, and the clams taste just as good.''

Raine was only getting the barest details of Cotter's explanation as her eyes focused on a pitchfork full of seaweed being tossed into a huge kettle. Her mind was trying to pull her back—back to this afternoon when she'd silently thought of Cotter with Anona. She grimaced inwardly. He had been thinking of her—and he hadn't wasted any time acting on his thoughts.

"Okay," Nordie was directing. "That's enough rockweed. Now for Miss Webber's clam contribution. Careful, Billy boy. These are the professor's."

A delicious whiff of steamy air wafted over them, and Raine realized how hungry she was. "They smell wonderful," she murmured to no one in particular.

"I can't wait to see your face when you have your first taste." Cotter's low remark sounded strangely sensual, startling her, and she cast a questioning, sidelong look up at him.

"I see you called Anona." Before she had any idea that she was going to say it, the wayward remark had escaped her tongue. Surprised at herself, she winced inwardly.

His gaze narrowed, his expression becoming meaningful as he murmured, "Anona and I think alike."

Raine couldn't draw her eyes away from his, dark and deep, for they neither caught nor reflected any light from the wildly dancing flames.

Chapter Seven

Raine flung a frustrated arm to shield her eyes from the bothersome moonlight. She knew that it was well past two, for the party hadn't broken up until after midnight. Her students, stuffed with steamed clams and exhausted, had exited hastily, knowing that the next day was a workday. Raine knew it, too, but still she tossed and turned, her mind swirling with images of Anona and Cotter, splashing around playfully in the surf. The memory gave her no peace.

She had spent most of her evening sitting quietly beside Carl, helping him open and remove the meaty clams from their shells, and trying to keep conversation on things that might interest him—and distract her. It hadn't worked. Her eyes and mind had continued to wander over the moonlit seascape for any glimpse of Cotter's broad, supple shoulders, or his startlingly light hair. Many times she had located him by the sound of his deep laughter, usually mixed with the light, musical sound of Anona's voice.

Groaning, she turned on her side, giving up, and stared toward the window, knowing that she wasn't going to get any sleep that night. She was too angry, disgusted with the envy she had discovered in herself. All that evening, during the party, she had grown more and more depressed, her anger focused on Cotter and his attentiveness toward Anona.

How could Raine Webber, a woman who had lived her whole life by clearheaded logic, suddenly become so irrational and flighty? Of all the men in the world to find herself in love with. Cotter Hunt was an egotistical playboy. It was the most absurd choice she could imagine. But the vision of Cotter's dark, expressive eyes lingered with her. And the memory of his provocative touch and stirring kisses surrounded her.

Distressed, she threw the covers aside and sat up, rubbing her eyes with trembling fingers. This self-absorbed attitude was becoming impossible, an impediment to her work. She simply must not torture herself with things that could never be. Cotter Hunt was a wealthy bachelor with a glamorous worldly girlfriend. It hurt to realize it, but she felt that knowing the truth would help her to redirect her energies. With a determined swing of her hand, she groped toward the bedside table for her glasses and the lamp switch. Maybe a good book...

Her hand grazed her glasses, knocking them off the table. By the clattering sound, she realized that they had tumbled toward the window. "Rats," she mumbled, dropping off the bed to her hands and knees, feeling around for them. "Must everyone and everything conspire against me tonight?"

A rattle outside her window distracted her from the search, and she listened apprehensively. The rattle came again, and she frowned, unable to make out what the sound was. It might have been a branch scraping the glass. But she was sure that there was no wind. Very cautiously, she moved her fingers, feeling along the floor for her glasses. She was more than a little handicapped without them. The cool, familiar feel of her frames nudged her little finger, and she quickly clasped the glasses up and put them on, blinking up toward the window. The curtains were drawn open, but all she could see was misty moonlight. Still on her knees, she crawled slowly toward the window, listening. The scratching was getting louder—but not loud enough to drown out the pounding of her heart as it hammered against her ribs.

When she was directly below the window, she reached up and curled her fingers over the marble sill. Very slowly, she raised up on her knees, lifting her head, eyes unblinking and wide, to peer outside. At first, she saw nothing. But after a few seconds, she could detect a little movement in the trellis beside the window. Another scratching, and she saw a dark gloved hand reach up and grasp the trellis.

Someone was climbing up the outside of the house! Her throat closed, and she couldn't move. To her horror, another hand appeared directly in front of her face. She strangled a scream that welled up in her throat as the hand grabbed the window ledge. Good Lord! Someone was trying to get in her window!

Her hands grew slick and gave up their hold on the sill as her fear-weakened knees gave way, and she sank to the floor. She wanted to shriek, but no sound would come. She found herself crawling awkwardly away, keeping low, forcing herself to stay alert as she heard a new sound. The sound of chalk on a blackboard—or something sharp, cutting glass?

With all the courage she could muster, she scurried to the bathroom door, unlocking it. Fearfully, she gradually, soundlessly turned the knob, opening the door just enough to slither through. Then, and only then, did she rise to her feet and fly through Cotter's door, throwing herself down beside his bed. *"Cotter!"* she pleaded in a tight whisper. "Cotter, wake up!" She shook his shoulder. "Hurry! Please."

"What—" He ran a hand through his tousled hair, opening one eye. "I must be slipping." He squinted a sleepy smile. Lifting a hand to her pajama lapel, he added with an unhurried yawn, "I've never dreamed about a woman wearing those before."

She brushed his hand away and whispered urgently, "Listen to me, Cotter. There's someone trying to—"

A buzzer went off on a complicated-looking console beside his bed and a light began to flash with the words: WINDOW VIOLATED: 13-2. At the same time, her room became flooded with light.

"Damn!" Wide awake now, Cotter threw his covers back and jumped out of his bed. Raine could only stare at the naked man as he grabbed up a robe, throwing it carelessly on as he bounded across his room toward her lighted one. The buzzer beeped in unison with the flashing words, but Raine could only gape at the empty door through which his muscular frame had disappeared. She heard nothing, and her heart rose in her throat. "Cotter?" she called. "Cotter? Are you—"

"I'm fine. Just a minute." In four quick strides he was back beside the bed, flicking off the alarm. And as quickly, he was at the nightstand, answering the ringing phone. "Yes. Hunt residence. No mistake. An attempted break-in. I saw only one man, dressed in black—or in dark clothes. No. Not the face. We're okay. Just a little cut glass. He's probably over the wall by now, considering how fast he was running. I know you'll contact me if you find anything suspicious."

When he hung up, the room was very still. Raine could hear him exhale heavily as he sat down beside her on the edge of the bed. "Police?" she asked in a shaky whisper.

He nodded, but seemed preoccupied as he sat forward, his elbows on his knees, apparently forgetting she was even there. Here she had not been able to sleep for thinking of him, and now, he was sitting beside her. She was in his bed, but he was hardly aware that she was even there! She sighed, and began to slide her legs over the side of the bed. "Well, since everything's okay, I'll go...."

He started, turning around. "Oh." His tense expression softened. "Yes, everything's all right. We've had break-in attempts before. My alarm feeds directly into the police station. They'll send a car to patrol outside the grounds. So don't worry. You all right?"

She swallowed and nodded. "I think so. You?"

He shrugged a shoulder and his robe fell open to the waist. "Yes. Our would-be burglar is probably the one most damaged. The automatic lighting system probably scared a good bit of life out of him."

"Pretty sophisticated system." Trying to be conversational was almost more than she could muster.

He smiled faintly. "Apparently it would be a waste of money for someone like you. You're a light sleeper."

She averted his gaze. She had no intention of discussing her insomnia with him, so she merely nodded, agreeing quietly. "I guess. Well, I'd better go. It's not exactly appropriate for me to be here." Feeling a deep blush rush up her neck, she hurriedly moved toward the opposite edge of the bed.

"Before you go..." He turned just enough to take her wrist, halting her. "I suppose I should thank you for your single-minded attentions to Carl tonight. This is the first time since the accident he's stayed out of his room for a whole evening. No doubt that was due to you."

Raine blinked at the trace of rancor in his voice. She straightened. "There's no need to thank me. It was my pleasure."

She felt his fingers trace lightly over her own. He had released her wrist, and she knew that she was free to leave, but somehow, his touch held her securely. Wanting to prolong the contact, she improvised. "Besides, I didn't think you noticed, you were so—so totally occupied." She kept her eyes level with his, watching him warily.

"I noticed," he returned in a deep, low tone. "I imagine you and Carl have a lot in common—I mean, you're both educated, you both like football." One long finger traced back and forth over the sensitive skin of her palm, sending shivers of heightened feeling through her. After a brief pause, he asked softly, "I'm curious, professor. Do you get more pleasure from his intelligent conversation, or is it the fact that he's sick that attracts you?"

Her brows shot up at his suggestion. She had no intention of answering such a ridiculous question and began to get up, but a steely hand caught her wrist, pulling her back down. "Don't run away, professor. Fight that timidity of yours, and stay." His eyes were calculating, his features hard.

The blood rushed to her face, bringing scalding tears to her eyes. Angry beyond any experience she could remember, she tried to pull her hand away, biting out through clenched teeth, "I'll show you timidity!"

But before she could slap him, he caught her outflung hand, murmuring quietly, "At least a man like me can arouse your passionate temper."

"That *would* be your idea of an accomplishment!" she challenged.

"You mean my uneducated idea of an accomplishment, don't you?" he corrected.

"Oh, come off it. I'm tired of it!" she returned hotly. "Your fixation about diplomas, your complete involvement with your so-called inadequacy, is sicker than anything about Carl!"

He cocked a brow. "Oh?" His lips quirked cynically. "That's easy to say when you've had an education given to you on a silver platter. When nobody's called you—"

"*Names?*" she finished for him in a shrill whisper. "I thought we've been through that, Cotter. So you didn't go to college. It's not a tragedy." She threw out an expansive arm. "Look what you've got. More than my folks—both college teachers—could ever have!" She took a deep breath and her eyes glittered. "Just what is it that you're lamenting? You should be proud of what you have, and how you got it. Who wouldn't be proud of the status you've achieved? I'll bet you my Ph.D. there's something else you're obsessed with, Cotter."

He put a finger to her lips, halting her heated speech. "Okay, okay," he said softly. "We don't need everybody coming in here taking sides in this debate." He tilted his head slightly to one side, a crooked smile softening his features. "You know, I think you're winning in the fight against timidity." There was a twinkle in his dark eyes.

Raine flushed but couldn't restrain a shy smile. His sudden easy humor was too infectious to ignore.

He grinned at her, tipping her chin up so that she was forced to meet his gaze. A low laugh rumbled deep in his throat. "Professor, if anybody had told me a woman could spend twenty minutes in my bed, and all we'd do is compare childhood wounds, I'd have thought they were nuts."

Her smile faded, and she lifted her chin away from his warm touch. She *would* be the one woman he could utterly resist—even in his bed.

"Tell me, do you actually sleep in those?" He cocked an appraising eyebrow.

Startled by his abrupt change of subject, she lifted her shoulders defensively, sidestepping his question with her own. "They're pajamas. What's so strange?"

He chuckled softly. "I wasn't referring to the pajamas." She felt fingers curling around her glasses frames. "I meant these. You don't sleep in them, do you?"

"Of course not, I—"

"Oh, yes, you grabbed them when you heard the prowler. Very resourceful. Quick thinking, too."

That sounded like as good a reason she could have thought up, so she let it pass.

"May I see them?"

"Why?" Her eyes grew wide with surprise. "They're just glasses."

"I guess it's not really the glasses I want to see. It's you, without them." As he spoke, he took them off, laying them on the bedside table. "There." He smoothed a stray strand of hair away from her eyes, murmuring, "Not a trace of schoolteacher left." He chuckled. "I feel as if I'm in a dream, finally allowed to uncover the beauty behind the glasses."

Blinking, she squinted a frown in his direction. She couldn't see his face clearly, and she wasn't sure she'd understood his quiet remark. Shifting restlessly, she held out a hand. "Cotter, give me my glasses. I can't find my way to my bed without them."

"Exactly." His fingers closed around her outstretched hand. "I don't want you to go."

"What?" she breathed the word almost fearfully.

"No, you're supposed to ask me why," he corrected.

She swallowed, easing the new dryness in her throat. "Why, then?"

Even as blurry as he was, she could see his shrug. "Because, I care for you. Because I've got you smiling at me again." He moved closer. "Because there's something about you, so that when you're away from me I feel as if I've lost something important." His moonlit face was now so close that he came clearly into focus. He was not smiling. "That's why."

"Be serious, Cotter," she pleaded in a soft whisper.

"But, Raine," Drawing her hand to his chest, placing it palm down in the dark mat of hair, he assured her, "I am serious."

She gasped at the feel of his taut muscles. He covered her hand, imprisoning it there. His chest rose and fell under her captured fingers as his breathing became rougher. "And those crazy pajamas, Raine. So much about you brings out some, I don't know, sort of protective instinct in me—but it's sensual and protective all at once." He looked deep into her eyes. "I want to show you things. Teach you things." His whisper grew husky. "I want to watch you come alive. I want us to share that, together." He slid a leg across her knees, easing her down on the bed. He lifted her other hand, kissing first the palm and then the sensitive skin on the inside of the wrist. "Stay,

Raine." He breathed the plea against her flesh. "Let me."

She groaned, closing her eyes. She had heard his soft, gentle urgings, but answered more to his sensual coaxing. Her fingers tangled themselves possessively in the thick hair of his chest, and she sighed, loving the coarse feel of it. "Oh, Cotter..." she began.

His dark eyes sparkled with a masculine determination that held her rapt. With lips now feathering her cheek, he continued, "I want you to feel more than compassion for me. There's so much more." His hip pressed suggestively against hers, and a persuasive hand went to the nape of her neck. Long, eager fingers stroked her short hair as she was guided beneath the cool sheets. A sigh of inescapable surrender was the only sound that could be heard in the room as his mouth closed possessively over hers. She loved him. And she could no longer deny her feelings for this man. She inhaled deeply, stimulated by his scent. His lips, too, were weaving their spell as he nuzzled and teased the soft flesh of her mouth.

His lips lifted from hers to move with deliberate slowness along her cheek to her neck. "You're a soft woman, Raine," he breathed. "I knew you would be." Searching fingers grazed her throat and moved slowly, tantalizingly, down to the first button of her pajama shirt. She inhaled sharply when the button slipped open. "It's okay," he murmured as his warm hand slid beneath the fabric to stroke her breasts. His moan mingled with hers, and his face moved down to replace the searching hand, to kiss her where he had awakened her flesh with his touch.

The shirt slipped away into the darkness, and Raine hugged his glistening head to her chest. Her head lolling back, she reveled in the feel of him; his hard, matted chest against her stomach, his square jaw exquisitely defined and rough against her body. She kneaded the muscles in his shoulders and back as he caressed and explored her soft, secret places. She tried to find the words to express her emotion, but her thoughts were blocked with the wonder of his touch and the dark sensuousness of his eyes.

Raine realized with a quiver of anticipation that he had eased the rest of her clothing away from her. Dismissing all thoughts, she pressed against him, loving the feel of his powerful body against hers. She discovered the potency of his desire as it teased the inner side of her thigh. And she marveled at the depth of her own feeling, finding herself responsive to his every nuance and every gesture.

Rising above her, Cotter stretched his sinewy shoulders and arms in the moonlight as he lifted his body to meet hers. At his intimate touch, she gasped, closing her eyes to all else but the ecstasy of their joining.

Her head rocked back and forth and she flicked at his lips and met his tongue with her own. Her breathing quickened as their tempo increased catapulting her toward a plane of pure pleasure and explosive light. She knew that she was near the edge, and she reached up to discover what was to come. Relishing the suspense, she met him equally, with a graceful, rhythmic dance of her own, enhancing their coupling beyond her control until she uttered a tremulous moan. Her body seemed to burst with rapture, surging with fulfillment. She curled her arms around Cotter's back as he lowered himself to cover her. Tears of happiness filled her eyes and she experienced the gratifying delight of his convulsive climax.

"Raine" he cried, pulling her into him, his arms trembling, tightened about her. "Raine..."

She squeezed her eyes shut, smiling at the loving, almost incredulous tone in his voice. A tear rolled across her temple and he softly kissed the damp trail that marked its passing. Raising his hand, he smoothed a strand of hair from her cheek. "What came over us...?"

She opened her eyes, her lips quivering in a smile. "Don't you know?" The teasing lilt of her voice seemed unnaturally playful, and she wondered at herself—at what had come over *her*. Cotter, certainly, had known this passion before, but for her it was new and incomparable. Flushing, her smile grew stronger with the memory. "Cotter?" she murmured, reaching for his shoulder.

Another Man's Treasure

His eyes clouded with an unreadable emotion. "I'm sorry, Raine," he said, looking stricken. He rolled away from her, not stopping until he was hunched on the edge of the bed, his hand clasped behind his bowed head.

The mist of pleasure lifted from her brain, and she shivered with the loss of his warmth. Pulling the sheet about her body, she could only stare wide-eyed as he sat there, shaking his head slowly from side to side. "What have I done?" He looked up and stared unseeing out the window. "Professor Raine Webber. Sweet, book-smart, earnest, protected and protective. You're delicate, Raine, too delicate for a man like me. You teach, and nurture, and console, all in ways that I don't understand. You're beyond a man like me, Raine. What do I have to offer you? Compassion? Intrigue? I don't even know. I toss you on your back, when you've come to me for help. What kind of gesture is that?" he growled. "There are rules about what a man like me can do—how far I can go with a woman." He looked at her for a long moment before he shook his head. "You don't even know what I'm talking about, do you?" He didn't wait for her to answer. "What I'm saying is, I'm sorry. I'm no Prince Charming. Far from it. And I have no intention of becoming one. It's beyond me." He cleared his throat, but Raine cut in before he could finish.

Her lips began to tremble, but she began, "Cotter, I don't know who you think I am or what this means to us."

"Hell!" He raged just above a whisper as he swooped down over the edge of the bed. She moved aside, and he grabbed at her pajamas, lying rumpled on the floor. With self-disgust in his face, he tossed them to her. "Damn it! If I could take this night back, I would. You—you're nice, too nice." He stared into her eyes. "To be honest, you're nothing I've ever looked for in a woman before." He ran a hand through his tousled silver hair and Raine was surprised to see that his hand was shaking badly.

Shaking? The unreachable Cotter Hunt? Somehow, the realization seemed absurd, considering the almost absolute calm he projected most of the time. A strange sort of shock began to numb her mind and body. Cotter wasn't able to let himself feel for her—it uncovered something, some other feeling of his, that was just too powerful for him.

The illusions about him were destroyed quickly, at least. If she could be nothing to him, then she would try to feel nothing toward him. He blurred before her again, but this time she knew that some of the haze was due to the tears that shimmered in her eyes. Listlessly she gathered her pajamas and sat forward, pulling the shirt about her shoulders. She reached for her glasses, and put them on quickly. Seeing movement out of the corner of her eye, she shot an apprehensive glance toward him. He had leaned toward her, taking hold of the lapel of her shirt. He tried to help her back into the sleeve, but she brushed his hand away. "Don't..." She let the feel of his touch fade and then pulled her arm through the sleeve. Words cost her too much energy. She was buttoning the shirt, her fingers unfeeling but steady, when she felt his weight as he settled on the bed beside her. His low murmur seemed very near, yet very far away, as he said, "Raine, I'm sorry."

She held up a halting hand as she slid to the other side of the bed and stood up. With her pajama bottoms clutched tightly in a fist, she looked directly at him, working hard at keeping her voice from betraying her deep hurt as the numbness gave way to pain. "Yes. I know." She walked away and rested momentarily against the door frame before she turned abruptly. "I think..." she began, but paused to quell a sob that threatened to overcome her. "There shouldn't be any problem with my keeping my distance from you now, Cotter." She lowered her eyes, breaking any contact that remained between them.

She couldn't recall a thing after that—not her return to her room, not sliding into her own narrow bed. All that she could remember was the vision of his black, brooding eyes when he spoke to her.

She compared her pain to the hurt she had known before. A desolate feeling surfaced, and she turned to bury her face in her pillow. There was no comparison.

COTTER LAY ON HIS BACK, staring at the ceiling, wondering at his lack of self-control. He'd never done anything so thoughtless in his life. Raine wasn't the kind of woman who understood how it was with a man like him. She played for keeps. She would equate sex with love. What did she know about men and women and casual sex? To her, there was no such thing. Raine was the type of woman who wanted and needed commitment. He grimaced. She deserved a virtuous man. She was a lovely, honest woman, and she needed the same qualities in a man. But she didn't need Cotter. He'd worked hard to build up what he had; to keep his family together. And when he wanted a woman, he had no trouble finding one. But the relationships had no strings and no responsibilities. It was a simple arrangement, one he couldn't fathom changing.

He closed his eyes and searched his soul. Why had he sent Anona home after the party? She'd certainly made it clear that she wanted to stay. And why had he felt so uncharacteristically attracted to this innocent in men's pajamas?

He placed a heavy hand across his eyes, swearing at himself again. He didn't need that kind of complication. Let her find someone more appropriate—an academic or a social worker. She'd be fulfilled with the right man. He rubbed a hand over tightly closed eyes as a strange feeling of unease closed over him at the thought of Raine in the arms of some gentle, loving man—someone other than himself.

Frowning, he opened his eyes, letting his gaze drift toward the door she'd passed through some time ago. He saw her image clearly, standing there, in the oversized shirt, her slim legs white and shapely in the dappled moonlight. She really was a lovely woman. Strange that she seemed to take such pains to hide that fact. Suddenly, he found himself growing angry. She was probably even striking, but she wore no makeup to enhance her features—and those huge glasses! She seemed not to try....

His upper lip broke out in beads of sweat. Didn't try? The way she reacted to him in that bed, she didn't have to try. She was so genuine, so unsophisticated, so beautifully uninhibited—so easy to love.

He sat up, feeling uncomfortably aroused by the memory. He shook his head to clear the thought of it. He didn't need any woman compelling him, and didn't want it. He didn't want her. He'd told her so, and that was the end of it. He had all the responsibility he could handle, with Carl and Nordie and the business.

Swinging his legs over the edge of the bed, he picked up his alarm clock to peer at the time. It was nearly five. Good. Close enough to time to get up. A cold shower and the light of a new day was what he needed.

As he set the clock back down, something nudged his fingers. He winced, knowing instinctively what it was. Her glasses. With a scowl he picked them up, fingering the frames. Why was it that she could never completely leave a room?

Chapter Eight

Raine leaned back heavily against the sorting table wanting nothing less than to have to begin another day's work. Listlessly, without any thought, she tugged on her gloves, hoping the students wouldn't notice the redness in her eyes and the slight bluish cast to the skin just above her cheekbones. The early morning hours had been difficult, to say the least. She looked around, trying to concentrate on physical things in the cavernous stables—trying to blot everything from the night just past out of her thoughts. The memory of Cotter's lovemaking was just as painful to recall as his cruel rejection.

The students were in the process of taking their smocks from hooks and donning them. She cleared her throat to steady her voice, and to her consternation, she realized that they had all become silent and were turned toward her, waiting. Blanching, she cast about in her mind for something to say—after all, she was supposed to be their teacher, to direct them in their study. Clamping her hands around the edge of the sorting table, she improvised. "I wonder how many of you have noticed specific features of the buying differences between the high- and low-income groups, so far?"

Bill's face grew thoughtful, and he raised a gloved hand. "I may be mistaken, but it seems like lower-income families buy many more vitamins, for one thing."

Raine nodded and tried to smile. "That's one of the interesting facts that appears to correlate with studies done at the University of Arizona. Anything else?"

There was a pause before Nordie chimed in, "Educational toys!"

Raine was glad for the chance to think about something besides Cotter. Nodding toward Nordie, she coaxed, "What about them?"

"They buy more." Nordie picked up a torn container. "This held a 'Spell and Talk.' Yesterday I found a couple of pieces from a Scrabble game and a set of instructions out of a children's weather forecasting kit in the low-income trash. I haven't found that much educational stuff in a week in the high-income bags."

"Good observation. I've noticed a trend in that direction myself. Evidence of more educational toy purchases in the lower socioeconomic group seems surpising, but this is just the type of thing we're making this study for. To discover—"

A squeak of unoiled hinges intruded on her explanation, and all eyes turned to see Cotter and another man enter the stables. Raine felt her body go stiff, but her heart was far from still as her eyes clashed with Cotter's for a brief, tense instant. She adjusted her gaze to look at the other man and recognized him immediately. Slightly shorter and stockier than Cotter, dressed in a light-colored sport coat, a white sport shirt opened at the neck and dark brown slacks, he was the smiling opposite of the stern-faced Cotter, dressed in a trim-fitting grey three-piece suit. The curly-haired Police Detective Noonan nodded toward Raine in friendly recognition.

Feeling Cotter's eyes on her made it difficult to create the illusion of pleasantness, but she strained to produce a professional smile, which she directed toward the police officer. Extending a hand toward his outstretched one, she offered, "Why, Detective Noonan. It's nice to see you again. What brings you here?"

He squeezed her hand, his green eyes crinkling in a friendly grin. "Heard about your near run-in with an intruder at headquarters, so I figured I'd better get out here and take charge of your safety in person."

Her smile faded at the reminder of last night. Swallowing hard, she could not find an appropriate answer. But Nordie spared her the necessity. "Intruder!" She crossed in front of the detective and faced Raine directly. "What intruder? Why didn't I know about it?"

Raine opened her mouth to reply, but it was Cotter who answered. "Because it wasn't that important. The alarm system frightened him away before he got in Raine's window."

Nordie's melodramatic eyes widened. "Professor Webber's window?" She spun to face Raine. "You must have been terrified!"

Raine looked down at her sandals, pressing her glasses firmly on her nose with the back of her wrist. She cleared her throat. "Well, at first, but Cotter...the system...took care of it."

Nordie giggled. "I can just see him dashing into your room ready to do battle—lights going on everywhere." Raine looked back up at the girl just as she turned to face her brother. "Say, Cot. Do you still sleep in the raw?" She shook her head and laughed. "I'll never forget that time when I set that wastebasket on fire under the smoke detector in the hall—you remember when ex-Senator Ranton, his wife and daughter and some other people were visiting. I decided it would be fun to have a combination fire-drill-come-as-you-are party. You rushed out into the hall naked."

"That's enough, Nordie," Cotter broke in, his irritation evident. He crossed his arms before his chest and said nothing further as she turned a playful smirk toward Raine, and put a consoling hand on her arm.

"I hope the experience didn't damage you for life—and I don't mean the break-in."

"Nordie, what could I do to persuade you to keep your mouth shut?" Cotter growled, his dark eyes smoking a warning.

She shrugged an unconcerned shoulder. "Oh, you couldn't do that."

Raine stood there, red-faced, wishing she were invisible. Detective Noonan cleared his throat amid the sound of stifled laughter from the students. "This is what I've decided to do, and Mr. Hunt has okayed the idea, although reluctantly." He looked at Cotter, smiling almost apologetically. "I'm going to stay here for the next two weeks until your study is over. I'm afraid, even though Mr. Hunt is doubtful about it, that the break-in last night could have been directly related to our investigation. So, I'd rather stay here, just to make sure no important evidence gets taken."

Raine's eyes widened. That thought had never occurred to her. "But—but, I haven't found a thing that appears to be important. I've never even taken the box into the house." She swept a hand down to show the officer the grey metal box, lying open. A handful of paper scraps were scattered about the bottom. "And we don't keep this place locked at night."

Nordie smirked. "Anybody who'd want to steal this stuff would have to be pretty hard up."

"Or desperate," Cotter cautioned.

Raine cast a scant glance toward Cotter and was distressed to see his eyes on her. It was obvious that he was against the whole idea of their helping the police. But it was done, and right now she had no interest in pleasing him anyway. Stubborn pride strengthening her voice, she directed her students. "Well, people, break-in or no, it's time we got started. Detective Noonan, I gather, will stay here with us. So, let's get him a coat and gloves."

"Oh, formal?" the officer quipped lightly, drawing Raine's gaze. He was smiling warmly at her, his mossy-colored eyes twinkling with humor. He winked, and she felt color rush up her cheeks. He mentioned to her quietly, "You know what, Raine? I think I'm going to enjoy this assignment."

Cotter snorted derisively and Raine noticed that he hadn't smiled once since he'd entered with Ike Noonan.

"'Bye, Cotter." Nordie was gaily waving a limp glove clutched in her fist. "Collect a lot of trash today. I'm going shopping Saturday—at Diamonds-Are-Us."

Raine heard the big door squeak shut and knew that he was gone. Her tense back muscles eased a fraction, and she turned to help Ike on with his smock. When he realized what she was doing, he graced her with another wide grin. It was infectious. She smiled back at him, noting that he was quite an attractive man, with his sun-bleached hair, tanned skin and broad shoulders. He appeared to be a man who took good care of himself. As a policeman, he would probably have to. She held out a pair of blue rubber gloves. But instead of taking them from her as she'd expected, he took her hand in his, murmuring, "Thanks. How about taking a walk with me after dinner tonight? I bet the beach is lovely in the evening."

She raised surprised eyes to meet his, her mouth opening in a silent "Oh." She stammered shyly, "Well, I—I'd like to, Mr. Noonan."

He nodded, squeezing her hand slightly before he pulled the gloves from them. "Ike."

She turned away to open the first bag of trash, her brows coming together in a slight frown. Why did life have to be like this? Why did she have to want Cotter, think only of Cotter, cry desperately over his rejection of her, when a nice man like Ike Noonan showed such obvious interest? Ignoring the twisting knot in her stomach, she pulled a tuna can from the sack and began to explain to the detective their involved process of tabulation. He proved to be a quick, extremely attentive student. It was a shame, she thought to herself, that his interest only made her uncomfortable.

COTTER TOYED WITH THE STEM of his wineglass as Hanna cleared away the dinner dishes.

"Sir? Would you like a piece of my rhubarb-and-lemon pie?"

He shook his head without looking up. "No, thank you." He filled his glass from the wine bottle that was sitting in a silver ice bucket at his elbow. "I won't need anything else tonight. You ought to be going anyway."

She lifted the tray full of dishes and offered a subdued, "Yes, sir. Good night," and exited through the pantry door.

He took a sip of the wine, eyeing its clear color without interest. For some reason he was in a foul mood. If he were to be truthful with himself, he'd been uncharacteristically out of sorts since Raine had stalked out of his bedroom, four nights earlier. And that laughing hyena of a police detective hadn't made matters any better. He'd been prancing and bowing around her like a circus horse, laughing at everything she said as though she alone had invented the art of witty conversation.

He set the glass down, grinding his teeth at the memory of Ike's attentions to Raine all during dinner. It had been a repeat of every night before. He'd flung his arm casually across the back of Raine's chair through the whole meal, whispering clever remarks in her ear. They must have been clever, because Raine had smiled and blushed the whole time.

Cotter had bit his tongue more than once. As a matter of fact, she'd managed to fluster him every time her cheeks had gone pink. He wondered just what the guy had been suggesting. He took another swig of the wine. And they'd taken enough walks along the beach! One would have thought they'd seen the whole coast of Maine by this time. But, no. They were going again tonight. He took another large swallow, frowning.

"Well...you still here?"

Cotter lifted his head, turning cool eyes toward the man whose incessantly pleasant personality had begun to irritate him. "What?" He felt his jaw go tight with his effort not to remark that he was free to do so if he wanted to sit at his table until hell froze over.

Ike waved off the brisk question. "I won't bother you, I was just—"

"Looking for Raine," Cotter finished between clenched teeth.

Ike grinned ingratiatingly. "Yes. How did you know?"

Cotter carefully released his glass so as not to break the steam. "It just came to me."

"Well, she said she'd meet me here," the detective explained. "She went to the kitchen to get marshmallows. We're going to roast them down by the wild cranberry patch between some dunes—oh, I'd say half a mile.'' He cocked his head in the direction he was describing.

Cotter sat back curling his hands around the edge of the table. "I know where they are."

"Cot!"

Nordie came into view at the door, wheeling Carl before her. Her face was animated with happiness, and there was a strange, new sparkle of life in Carl's eyes. He sat up, alert. "What is it?" he asked, an edge of irritation still in his voice as he tried to prepare for any crazy possibility.

"You'll never guess—never in a trillion years—who's here!"

He lifted his eyes for divine guidance. "Nordie, just tell me."

She threw her arms wide. "Cammie! Cammie's come back!"

"Camille? Carl's—"

"Yes! Yes!" Nordie motioned for someone to come forward, whispering loudly. "Come on, Cam. Cotter won't bite you."

Camille Rathem Hunt stepped into the doorway as Nordie and Ike backed out of her way. She smiled tentatively at Cotter and, with a nervous gesture, tossed her long, red hair back over her shoulder. She seemed paler than he remembered, and a little thicker around the middle. The round face was drawn, and her light blue eyes were wary, even frightened. His frown faded, and he felt compassion overcome his anger. With a nod and a small smile, he stood up. "Hello, Cammie. To what do we owe the pleasure?"

She relaxed visibly with his unreproachful greeting, her smile growing stronger. "I've come to get Carl, Cotter. I've been doing a lot of thinking since I left—nearly three months' worth. And I have a lot more to think about." A sheen of guilty tears glistened in her eyes, and she pressed a handkerchief to her nose. "When he was disabled I panicked, you know?"

She paused, watching Cotter for a response. He nodded again. "I know. We all did."

Wiping at her eyes, she went on. "But yesterday, I talked to the doctor, and he said Carl's got a good chance to get back on his feet if he wants to. And if we work as a team, he can be walking that much faster." She put a hand on Carl's shoulder, and Cotter watched as Carl's hand moved up to cover it. "I'm going to need him to get on his feet as fast as he can."

Carl turned to look questioningly up at her.

She knelt beside him, lifting her arms to his neck. Barely above a whisper, she said, "I want you to be able to wheel me and our baby out of the hospital this Christmas."

"A baby..." Carl repeated.

The quiet that followed Cammie's announcement was solemn and heartfelt. No one dared interrupt the tacit promises that Cammie was making to her husband. They had obviously taken time to evolve, and the drama of the moment touched Cotter deeply.

The thump of a door beyond the pantry and the sound of Raine's beach scuffs broke the silence as she pushed through the pantry door from the kitchen. "Well, here they are..." She let the words die away, realizing that something very important was happening. "Oh, I'm sorry, did I interrupt...?"

Nordie clapped her hands together. "I'll say! I just found out I'm going to be an aunt." She gestured toward Cammie, who was coming to her feet. "Raine, meet Camille, Carl's wife. She's—" Nordie shrugged, glancing at Carl "—been away for a while, visiting her folks in Virginia, but now she's back."

Raine smiled at the fragile-looking redhead, surprised to see how young she was, probably only a year or so older than Nordie. "Well, that's wonderful news. I'm so happy for you both." She moved up beside Ike, handing him the bag of marshmallows.

Cammie pushed her hair back and smiled. "Thank you. I'm happy too.... We have a lot of work ahead of us, though."

Carl reached out and took her hand in his. "It's nothing we can't handle." Raine marveled at the new glitter of life in Carl's eyes as he gazed up at his wife, his face full of emotion. "I'd better get you home and take care of you." He motioned toward Nordie, and with a laugh that was completely unfamiliar to Raine, he said, "We've got to be going—Cammie and I have some packing to do. And tomorrow we've got to hire a cook so we can get back to our house in town."

"I'll take him. It's my turn." Cammie brushed Nordie's hands away from the handlebars. "Whatever you say, Carl."

She turned him around, and they headed off toward Carl's room. Raine was filled with the feeling of relief and hope for Carl and Cammie as she watched them leave together. What he'd needed was the continued support of his wife. It was reassuring to see that love could do more than hurt.

"Well." Ike draped his arm about Raine's shoulders. "That's marvelous." He squeezed her arm. "You about ready to go?"

Raine's eyes flicked to Cotter's face as she nodded her assent. She thought she had seen a spark of some dark emotion dash across his eyes with Ike's question, but she could have imagined it. His expression seemed placid enough as he watched Carl and Cammie disappear into Carl's room.

"Okay."

Ike led her toward the door. "See you folks later."

Nordie teased. "You two got any matches for a fire or are those marshmallows just a red herring to throw us off the scent of what you're really up to?"

Ike winked and laughed. Cotter sat down and poured himself another glass of wine.

"Well." Nordie stretched. "I'm tired. I'm going to bed soon. You, Cotter?"

"In a while," he muttered, lifting the glass to his lips.

"It's late. The guys have already turned in." She looked around, apparently checking to see if Raine and Ike were gone. She then tiptoed over to Cotter. "Say, don't you love the way Professor Webber and that good-looking cop are getting along? I mean, now that Carl's got Cammie back, don't you think it's great that she has a real live boyfriend?"

"You can't imagine how pleased I am," he muttered into his glass.

"And I feel totally responsible!" Oblivious to his glare, she leaned her hip on the table. "And you wanna know what I think? I think they're going to make it work, too. Isn't that exciting? My very own Professor Webber, with that fantastic-looking hunk."

Cotter shot to his feet, slamming his palms down on the table. The thunderous slap of his hands reverberated loudly in the quiet house. "I'm going to bed," he announced, barely above a whisper. With one long stride he stepped around Nordie and headed for the door.

"Cotter?" Nordie hurried after him, taking his hand. "What's with you lately? You bite everybody's head off for no good reason. I've never seen you so wound up."

"Nothing's with me." He inhaled slowly to compose himself, turning to meet her inquiring gaze. "I'm just tired. Okay?"

She cocked her head, squinting at him as though she didn't believe him. "Okay, so don't tell me." She let go of his hand, patting his arm as she offered gently, "Go to bed and have sweet dreams."

He thought of his own bed; thought of the last three nights, and the dreams he'd sweated through. He'd imagined a woman with short brown hair and huge, appealing eyes. She'd been wearing a suit of armor that looked strangely like a pair of pajamas—and there was a self-satisfied cop who kept appearing out of nowhere to carry her off into a mist, winking at Cotter over his shoulder. By no stretch of the imagination could those dreams have been categorized as "sweet." Unwilling to share his thoughts, Cotter pivoted away from his sister and strode out of the room.

DRIFTWOOD, DRY REEDS AND STICKS made a nice fire. It flickered and danced in the slight breeze as Raine shook her head at Ike's offer of another marshmallow. "No." She smiled, putting a hand on her stomach. "I've had plenty. Thanks."

He sat back on the thick patch of cranberry vines and rested on his elbows. "I've had enough, too, I guess." She could only make him out dimly as he looked around. "It sure is pretty here. Must be great to own a place on the ocean."

Raine shrugged noncommittally. "I'm sure it is." She wasn't particularly interested in the conversation, and her mind wandered to Ike's inconsistent behavior these past three days. When they were around other people, he acted as if he were absolutely smitten with her. But as soon as they were alone together, his manner changed, and he behaved more like a companion on a plane trip, chatting casually about any mundane subject just to pass the time. So far, they'd covered the weather in June versus the weather in September; current movies and their relative merit; a variety of sports events—apparently any insignificant topic that came to his mind would do.

Nor had he tried to kiss her, which seemed odd, because each day he'd whispered sexual innuendos that were beginning to make her terribly uncomfortable. Actually, she was just as glad he hadn't tried anything, because she would have hated to alienate the man who was supposed to be protecting her. Whatever the reasons for his strange behavior, she certainly couldn't fathom it. And with her nerves frayed over Cotter's gruff treatment of her lately, she didn't have the mental energy to spend much time worrying about it. She sighed quietly, nodding, hoping that the action was consistent with what he was saying. With determination, she tried to concentrate on his words.

"You do?" He seemed surprised, and she winced, wondering what he'd asked. He picked one of the cranberry plant's blossoms, a small, pink flower, and examined it closely. "I don't think it looks like a crane's head at all. Maybe I don't have enough imagination. Oh, well..." He tossed it carelessly into the breeze, sat up and twisted a knot in the top of the marshmallow bag.

Raine breathed a sigh of relief. He'd just been questioning the etymology of the word "cranberry." She didn't care if it came from "crane" or "football"; the issue wasn't a vivid one for her. Shifting her gaze toward the fire, she noticed the last flames were flickering out.

"Well, I guess we'd better get back," he said and he bounded athletically to his feet. "You look like you're getting a little chilled."

She wasn't. But she pulled her sweater closer about her shoulders and acquiesced silently as he helped her up.

"It was a nice, peaceful weekend. But tomorrow's another workday."

Raine agreed with a nod. "I hope, for the police investigation's sake, we find something useful soon."

He shrugged his husky shoulders as they walked. "Maybe there isn't anything to find. Maybe this guy's not guilty. It happens."

She considered that. "But, I thought..."

"Oh—" Ike shook his head, but continued to look ahead "—I believe he is. Don't get me wrong. And I want to be the guy to get him. We'll find something."

Raine heard a strange undertone of malice in his voice that made her turn to him, surprised. He seemed to be looking at something deep within himself, his expression self-absorbed. She lifted a questioning brow. This Ike Noonan was a curious, complex man. She would have given a lot to know what was on his mind at that moment, but for some reason, she couldn't bring herself to ask.

Once inside the house, Raine flicked the switch that set the alarm system. One dim light had been left on at the top of the stairs. She felt an odd sadness clutch at her throat and couldn't face dragging herself up to her dark, lonely room. Looking for an excuse, she caught sight of the half-full sack of marshmallows. "Oh—" she took it from Ike's hand "—I'll just put these away. You go on up."

He seemed at ease with the idea and grinned at her. "Okay. See you tomorrow. Bright and early."

Her smile wasn't as strong. "Bright and early. Good night." Making a hasty exit, she passed the formal living room and hurried down the hall and into the kitchen. She was not particularly surprised to see light seeping out from beneath the door. Hanna usually left a light on, so Raine didn't expect to find anyone there.

She pushed the door open, and a pair of dark eyes met hers. They were so hard, so unyielding, that she almost left at once.

"Evening." Unsmiling, Cotter took a bite of his sandwich before laying it down on a plate.

She swallowed, pulling her lips between her teeth. "I'll just—" she walked forward far enough to lay the marshmallows on the table, planning a hasty exit "—I'll just leave these and go...."

He swallowed the bite. "Have a nice time?"

"Yes." It was such a low whisper that she barely heard it. She doubted that he'd heard it at all.

"Good." He favored her with a doubtful half smile.

His chair scraped along the wood floor as he abruptly stood up. "How were the marshmallows?" As he clinched his robe more tightly at the waist, his eyes dropped to the bag on the table. "Or did you just dump them in the fire for the effect?"

Her gaze flitted from his face to the table. She was confused and annoyed now. What possible effect could she achieve by dumping a half bag of marshmallows into a fire? She pressed the back of her wrist to the bridge of her glasses, pushing them into place, repeating the word without comprehension. "Effect?"

"Never mind," he replied, as dark, angry eyes did a critical survey of her body. Without another word, he bent down to pick up his plate and crossed to the sink.

She felt a flare of resentment. He had no right to be rude to her. Maybe she wasn't what he wanted in a woman, but that wasn't her fault. She didn't know what sophisticated, experienced women like Anona knew, but she certainly hadn't pretended to. She had gone to Cotter on her own terms. It wasn't fair that Cotter blamed her and stalked around like a wounded animal, just because she hadn't been *visibly* hurt after his rejection of her. She clenched her fists tightly.

She felt uncomfortable with her own anger but lifted a proud chin to quell the trembling of her lips. "Cotter..." She was surprised to discover that her voice was firm. She paused, not quite knowing how to articulate what she wanted to say. When the silence weighed between them, he turned back to face her.

"Yes?" He eyed her doubtfully.

"I don't like being at odds and I don't intend to fight with you. But I want the air cleared between us," she began carefully. "I don't understand why you're acting this way. I've done nothing—" she cringed inwardly at the phrase and the way it came out, like a confession, but she forced herself to go on "—nothing to hurt you. You're acting like a spoiled child, and I don't think that's fair."

His eyes flashed and he allowed his emotions to show—his features became beautiful, yet fearsome. A muscle began to pulse in his jaw, but he said nothing. She saw a pained sort of contempt in his eyes as they raked over her, and it stung. His mouth tightened and he dropped his gaze as he turned his back on her. With an irritated flick of his wrist, he turned on the water. "However, Ike got what he expected, no doubt." His bitter remark was filled with scorn. It was evident by the set of his shoulders that she had been dismissed.

She stared blankly at the rhythmic movement of his shoulders as Cotter washed the plate and put it on the counter. Ike? What did he have to do with this? She frowned in thought. Then, as she absorbed his meaning, a new, unforeseen fury exploded in her. She finally understood what he'd meant by "effect." He was implying that she and Ike had made love!

Her expression of rage came out like a wildcat's growl, making Cotter swing back, to see her stalking toward him. "Why you egotist! You feel hurt, so you want to hurt and embarrass me! But I have news for you, Cotter. You've misjudged me...and it isn't going to work."

He raised his hand to ward off her anger. For the second time that evening he had arrived at the absolute wrong conclusion—instead of slapping him, she stomped on his bare foot, wishing her sandal had football cleats. Shocked by her attack, Cotter leaned against the counter and stifled a moan as Raine marched from the kitchen.

Chapter Nine

After a painful moment, Cotter looked toward the kitchen door. It was still swinging slightly on its hinges where Raine had pushed through. He sat down and, with great care, lowered his throbbing foot to the floor, bending forward to lean heavily on his forearms.

Closing his eyes, he recalled the sounds of light laughter and contented murmurings he'd heard from Carl's room when he'd passed by earlier. He should have been happy for Carl, and he planned to be, tomorrow. But, right now, the memory of those intimate sounds made him uneasy. Why? Certainly he wasn't jealous of his brother's situation—jealous that Carl had a wife who loved him, no matter what? It was true that Cammie had left Carl, but she had been very young and frightened when Carl got hurt. Now she was back, and it looked as though she had made the decision to stay and to help her husband.

He ran his hands through his hair and looked down at the tabletop. Raine's face flashed in his mind, and immediately after hers came the image of Ike's. He banged his fist on the table. "Hell!" he muttered.

The door swung open. "You called?" Nordie poked her head in and smiled. "Hi. Can't you sleep, either?"

He frowned.

She giggled. "Oh, good. You're glad to see me." She walked inside, letting go of the door. "Want to share a little leftover duck?" Tugging at the tie of her red silk robe, she headed for the industrial-size refrigerator. "I don't know why I'm hungry. I had plenty at dinner. But I just got this craving for some duck and a glass of grape soda."

He grimaced, his eyes following her. "Are you out of your mind?"

She laughed, her back to him as she fished around in the refrigerator. "Darling brother, I'm crazy like a fox." She pulled out the platter of duck and a can of soda. "Want some?"

He shook his head.

She set the plate down on the table and flipped the can open. It hissed and sprayed him. "Oops. Sorry." She pulled out a chair. "Why are you up?"

He eyed her warily, replying, "I can't sleep. And you?"

She picked up a piece of duck and waved it around. "It's the noise coming from Carl's room. All that heavy breathing." She rolled her eyes.

Cotter exhaled slowly. "Is nothing sacred with you?"

"Guess not." The corners of her mouth lifted in a smile as she took a swallow of her soda.

He looked away, not wanting to dwell on the subject of Carl.

"Speaking of love—" she was munching on another bite of duck "—I passed Professor Webber in the hall. Boy, was she flushed! You wanna bet why?"

He returned her look. When there eyes met, she winked. "The cop and the professor did it. Don't you think?"

He toyed with the soda can on the counter and barked, "Will you just eat and go to bed."

She cocked her head sideways, eyeing him curiously. "Why do you keep getting annoyed every time I mention those two? What difference could it possibly make to you if they're making whoopee?"

"It doesn't matter to me," he growled, running a fist along his jaw. "Why would it matter to me? Eat."

"I don't know, but..." She pulled on her upper lip with her teeth, watching him silently.

The cunning look in her eyes made him grow uncomfortable. His sister's thought processes could be convoluted when she set her mind to it. He had no idea what ridiculous conclusions she'd arrive at.

"Cotter?" Looking thoughtful, Nordie scratched her nose with her fingernail. "You know? For twenty-one years I've been trying to get your goat. But now, suddenly, you burst into flames every time Professor Webber and her love life crop up in the conversation." She nudged his shoulder with her elbow. "Why, even that time I told the mayor you'd miss his meeting 'cause you'd been arrested for telling state secrets, you didn't get this crazy." She eyed him with lips pursed in exaggerated contemplation. "Why would you say that is, Cotter?"

He clamped his jaws tight, scowling at her this time. Her smile didn't fade, and she leaned forward, resting her chin on folded hands. "Hmm." She pursed her lips, pondering the source of Cotter's anxiety. "Hmm..."

"What are you trying to say?" he ground out.

She grinned. "Nothing." She took a bite of her food and put it down. "It is funny, though. I mean, she does seem pretty partial to the cop." Nordie's eyes glistened with fun. "I can't imagine why. I mean, just because he's gorgeous, cheerful, and he dotes on her every word. How could she prefer him to you? After all, aren't you the conceited jerk of her dreams?

"Egotistical," he amended through clenched teeth.

"Huh?" She wrinkled her nose in question.

"Never mind." He shook his head, sighing. "Are you through?"

"Not quite." She dismissed him with a toss of her head. "I mean, you've lied to her and made a fool out of her—"

"All my idea, of course," he interrupted curtly.

She shrugged but went on, undaunted. "You glower, growl and stare at her as though you were about to command, 'Off with her head.' How could she choose Detective Noonan's boring consistent courtship over your innovative advances?"

"Advances! Now, that is crazy!" He bolted up. "I'm going to bed!"

Her high-pitched laughter followed him all the way down the hall.

Before he knew it, Cotter was standing inside his darkened bathroom rapping on Raine's door. He drew his hand back as though he'd touched molten lead when he heard her ask, "What do you want?"

He didn't know. Lowering his hand, he stared at the blank panels, unable to think of a plausible answer.

She repeated the question a little louder this time. "What do you want, Cotter?"

Feeling like a fool, he turned away, muttering gruffly, "Nothing. Go back to sleep."

Before he'd reached his door, he heard hers open. He knew she was standing there, watching his back.

He could picture Raine in her outlandish pajamas. She said nothing. After a long, palpable silence, he turned to face her, unable to help himself.

She was standing with one hand resting on the doorknob as though she expected to have to slam the door shut at any instant. Her face was solemn, questioning, closed in a slight frown. He was surprised to see that she wore only the pajama shirt. Even so, it draped her hips modestly. Cotter preferred not to be reminded of her graceful body, not now, anyway. He didn't have any idea what he wanted to say to her, he just knew he had to communicate something. Of course, Nordie was quite wrong. He wasn't jealous of Raine's interest in Ike Noonan. But he had to admit it made him unhappy to see her wary and distrustful—especially knowing he'd been the one to make her that way.

Considering everything, he owed her an apology. With a regretful air he offered quietly, "I hope you can forgive me for the other night."

Her expression didn't change, but for the slight arching of one brow. "I'm afraid it's a little late for that." She spoke calmly, clearly, without emotion. She looked very proud, very hurt—lovely and vulnerable. With an accusatory finger pointing at his chest, she said quietly, "You suggested things about me tonight that I can't forgive easily. So I've decided it would be best if we kept clear of each other until I leave next week. I can't see that there's anything left for us to say." With a brisk step backward, she quickly closed the door between them.

Her abrupt withdrawal took Cotter off guard. He'd expected her to be forgiving, to offer him a shy little smile. Why did she suddenly have to become self-righteous? He felt disappointed, and that, too, annoyed him.

She was wrong. There *were* things worth saying. And he wanted them said. He headed toward her door and took hold of the knob. Twisting it, he almost ran into the door when it didn't open. She had locked it. Rattling the knob, he called her name. Twice. Three times. But there was no response. The urge to bang on the door was almost too strong to ignore. But he controlled his urge, wishing he could find an outlet for his frustration.

Inhaling slowly, he regained a sense of calm. Trying for rational communication, he lifted his hand from the knob and held it out placatingly toward the blank door. "Look, Raine. If it's what I said about you and Ike—I didn't mean that." Suddenly he was not just saying that. He knew he hadn't meant what he had said to her earlier. She was not the type to get involved with a man so cavalierly.

Something thudded against the door, making him wince. Apparently she meant what she'd said. She was through speaking to him. He'd gone one step too far, even for a forgiving, protector-of-the-underdog like her. Dropping his head, he realized he couldn't blame her for the way she felt. He peered at the panels for a long moment, listening for any sound on the other side. There was only silence. Slowly he turned away, walking back into his big, dark room.

Cotter felt numb. He'd hurt Raine badly, and he'd also hurt himself.

With an irritated motion he unfastened his robe, shrugged out of it and, in one sweeping gesture, he picked it up and threw it across the room.

RAINE PULLED OFF her rubber gloves and checked her watch. It was four-thirty. Laying the gloves on the plywood table, she put her hands to the small of her back and stretched. It had been a long, difficult day. And a long, hard night. She tried to shake off the thought of her last sight of Cotter, just before she'd closed the door on him. She'd been trying to rid herself of the vision all day long. He'd been watching her with a vivid and penetrating gaze, studying her cautious expression. She hadn't been able to stand that devastating look for a moment longer. Her heart had been pounding, her body aching with the need to be held in his arms. She wanted him, but found herself unable to cope with his many contradictions. She couldn't accept him on the current terms—not even after he'd taken back his insinuations about her and Ike. But at least she did feel that he really had meant that.

Sighing, she looked around her. She'd already dismissed her students, and they were ambling out in a group, talking and laughing, and looking forward to the party in honor of Carl and Cammie. Nordie had explained its purpose as a farewell party that they were sure Cotter wouldn't think of having if left to his own devices.

Nordie had taken her lunch into Cotter's den and helped Cammie make all the necessary calls. And, by the time she'd gotten back to work at two o'clock, the party was definitely on. Dinner to be catered et cetera. Raine was surprised at how rapidly something that seemed so elaborate could be planned. She guessed that with enough money, one could do almost anything.

"Professor Webber?"

Raine's head jerked around at the sound of Nordie's questioning call. "Yes?"

"Remember—eight o'clock sharp. Casual. It'll be out by the pool, so you can swim, or dance, whatever."

Raine smiled politely, wishing she could beg off without having to defend her reasons. She was sure she'd get an argument from Nordie, and it hardly seemed worth the effort. So she merely nodded. "Eight sharp. Fine." She had no intention of going. Cotter would be there. She'd decline at seven-thirty with a convenient headache.

Nordie waved and disappeared out the door, leaving Raine alone with Ike, who was helping her off with her smock. "I don't know, I'm not happy about this party idea," he said.

Raine turned to face him as he took both of their smocks to the two empty hooks on the wall. She felt like saying he'd taken the words right out of her mouth. But she opted for the obvious question. "Why?"

He shrugged. "Never know who'll sneak in with the guests and poke around where he has no business."

Raine dropped her gaze to the metal box. "You don't think anyone could be after this stuff?"

He walked back to her side, taking her elbow. "Don't know. But I think I'll keep a pretty low profile. And I've already asked Nordie to tell her friends to refer to me only as your date. Nothing about my being a cop. Too many questions can come from that."

She nodded. "Okay. Low-profile date." Even in her dispirited mood, that struck her funny and she managed a smile. "How do you do that, crawl around under the chairs asking, 'Where's Raine, my date?'"

He chuckled, pushing the tall door open for her. "That's a good one. You surprise me sometimes." He closed the door firmly and resumed his hold on her elbow as they walked toward the main house.

"I'll probably just mingle a little, stand in dark corners, and watch and listen."

She nodded. "I see. What do you want me to do?"

He grinned at her. "You?" Squeezing her arm, he said, "You just have a good time and smile at me every once in a while. That way I'll feel less like I'm working."

Her smile was more one of embarrassment than anything else. And so was her blush. He was doing it again, acting as though he had a romantic interest in her. By now, she knew it was only an act. But she went along with it out of habit. Still smiling, she lifted her eyes to the cloudless sky and watched the swoop of a gull before she answered. "Have fun and smile. That sounds easy enough." On the other hand, when she thought about it, having fun and smiling in the context of being around Cotter Hunt might not be so easy, after all. She'd have to work on that headache.

EIGHT O'CLOCK SHARP. Raine looked at herself in the mirror. With her fingers, she smoothed her hair behind an ear, listening to the doorbell chime every few minutes. It sounded as though it was going to be a big bash.

Casual. She looked at her white cotton slacks and pink button-down, short-sleeved shirt. Not exactly elegant. But it did fit the description "casual." Nordie and Cammie had dropped by her room earlier,

Nordie in a hand-knit sweater of brilliant multicolored ribbons and bows and orange calfskin trousers, Cammie in an understated shirtdress and a lightweight jacket. Somehow, when Raine had been about to explain about her headache, she just couldn't do it. She was a coper, in the end. Prevaricating just wasn't her style.

Just as Raine reached the bottom step of the winding staircase, Anona flowed in through the front door, looking sleek in a pewter-colored jumpsuit. She was alone. With a smile of recognition, she swept over to Raine. "Why, hello." Her slanted eyes glowed with delight. "Isn't this fun? I was happy to hear about Cammie and Carl, though I've never really seen them together. Cotter and I didn't start dating until May." She rested a manicured hand on Raine's. "Speaking of Cotter, where is he?"

Raine didn't know and didn't want to know. She scanned the foyer, her gaze passing over the groups of guests that had not yet made it out onto the patio in back. "I don't see him, Anona. Maybe he's already by the pool."

Anona's eyes had been moving around the room, never quite focusing on Raine's. Now they paused at the double doors that led onto the patio, decorated with paper lanterns. "Well, I guess I'll go see." Finally her eyes met Raine's. "Good to see you." Before Raine could answer, she was gone.

As Raine stood there trying to decide where to go, the front door opened abruptly without the usual chime. "Cotter..." She breathed, surprised, and then clamped her lips closed when she realized she'd spoken his name aloud.

He stopped rummaging in a leather folder and lifted his eyes to hers. She suddenly became aware that all the guests that had been milling around her moments ago were now gone, and only she and Cotter were left in the brilliantly lit foyer. But the sounds of the party carried through the open doors.

He frowned. "What's going on?"

Apparently no one had told him about the festivities. Dressed in a silver suede jacket, black slacks, white shirt and black tie, he was obviously not prepared for a casual party. Raine regretted being in the position of telling him what his sister had arranged.

"Raine, please speak to me," he persisted, his expression solemn.

She relented slightly. "You don't know?"

He shook his head. "Why should I? It's only my house." A tired smile formed on his lips, and it was too melancholy to resist.

"Party. Combination baby announcement and going-away."

His brows lifted. "Oh." Slipping the leather folder under one arm, he inquired, "Is it formal, or Western, or is Nordie giving another one of her come-as-you-would-be-if-you-were-a-schizophrenic parties?"

"Casual." She pretended to gaze at a group of guests gathering in the living room.

"I see." His voice had grown much closer now, and she sought out his face for safety's sake. It was best to know where this man was at all times. He was shaking his head, seemingly at the evening's planned entertainment. "I'd better change. Would you tell my sister the telephone has finally been perfected? Next time, I'd appreciate knowing in advance when we're entertaining."

She nodded, dropping her eyes to the polished banister behind him. He'd taken one step up and was now on a level with her. She could feel the heat of his body near her and caught the scent of his mild cologne. She had been about to hurry away to a safe distance when she felt his fingers curl around her wrist. Her eyes darted to his.

He smiled hopefully. "I know I'm not a particularly smart man. But if you'll forgive me, I promise I won't work so hard at being stupid anymore." He was keeping his tone carefully neutral. "And if you can't forgive me, could you possibly speak to me in complete sentences?" He waited, his fingers firm and warm against her skin.

What were her alternatives? A surge of energy passed through her body as a result of his light touch. It weakened her resolve. Witty, soft words. They worked for a man with a face and body like Cotter Hunt's. She almost resented his charisma; it seemed to go against her logical interpretation of the world. But here was a man who could be logical and bright, but devastatingly emotional as well—when he let himself be.

She tensed against him, not wanting to be vulnerable to him yet again. She disengaged herself from his light grasp, adjusting her gaze toward the double doors of the patio. His face was a blur of highlighted angles but she didn't allow him to come into focus. With carefully spoken words, she told him, "Anona is looking for you."

As she walked away, she heard him murmur, "Thank you." For an instant, she had the distinct feeling that he was thanking her for the complete sentence rather than the information about Anona. When she stepped out into the cool of the evening, she shook her head, a humorless chuckle escaping her lips. Of all the foolish ideas she'd had about Cotter since she'd met the man, that was the stupidest yet.

COTTER WAS ALL TOO CONSPICUOUS that evening, dressed in white slacks and a white shirt. Ike, in black, was almost invisible. Cammie remained flushed and smiling throughout the festivities and, interestingly enough, so did Carl. Raine discovered that Carl had a hearty, deep laugh, much like his brother's. And when he was animated, Carl was almost as handsome as his brother.

Anona chattered and laughed all evening, too, but somehow, to Raine, the laughter eventually took on a hollow, false sound. Cotter seemed to be avoiding Anona, but she pursued him wherever he went.

Raine had never seen so much food, including delicacies she'd never before tasted; some were delicious and others merely exotic. Expensive champagne accompanied the feast. The students, under Nordie's watchful eye, were careful to drink little and stay sober, for, Nordie reminded them brightly, the following day would be another workday.

It was nearly midnight when Cammie and Carl finally said good-night to the departing guests and Cammie pushed Carl's wheelchair down the ramp and into the waiting car.

Fifteen minutes later, Raine was sitting on the wide marble railing, watching the low waves glisten in the moonlight as they moved silently over the sand. It was a beautiful night, crisp and still. Nordie's voice, hailing her from a distance, broke the spell. "Professor Webber?"

She turned. "Hi!" Raine's smile faded as she saw the young woman limping toward her. "What happened?"

Nordie shrugged. "Tripped on the front steps. Women's high-fashion shoes are death traps. Hey, could you give me a hand?" She leaned heavily on the railing.

"Sure." Raine hopped down. "What do you need?"

Nordie smiled pitifully, sweeping a hand toward the table that had served as a bar. "Could you carry these empty champagne bottles down to the cellar for me? The caterers cleaned up their own mess but the wine was ours, and like a dummy, I sent Hanna and Lys with Carl and Cammie to help them get set up, so there's nobody else to do it."

"The cellar?" Raine was a little surprised that she didn't just want the bottles discarded.

Nordie bent down and groaned, unbuckling the strap of the high-heeled shoe on her injured foot. "Uh-huh. We recycle everything."

With a shrug, Raine began picking up the bottles. "Okay. How do I get to the cellar?"

Nordie straightened and began flexing her foot. "Just go through the kitchen. It's the door on the left. There are some stairs, and then when you get into the basement, it's the door with a little barred window right beside the steps."

Arms full of bottles, Raine turned, a quizzical smile parting her lips. "Barred window?"

Nordie grinned. "That's where we keep all our valuable wines and our most deranged family members. Cotter keeps threatening to put me down there, but I think he knows I'd get revenge by drinking everything dated before 1850—which is only two bottles." She lifted the injured leg to stretch it along the rail. "It's not much, but they'd sure give me an expensive hangover."

Raine laughed. "Nordie, you're not a person, you're an experience."

"I know." She stretched like a contented cat. "Say, thanks for your help. It's a dirty job, but somebody has to do it." She twirled her foot. "I think it's getting better already. Maybe I should help."

"Oh, don't bother. You take it easy. I can manage."

Nordie turned away to scan the undulating seascape. "Well, if you're sure."

Raine found the basement door and trudged down the flight of stairs under the dim light of a single bulb. The door with the barred window stood ajar and a light glowed from inside.

She shifted the bottles into a better position as she entered the room. It was small, perhaps eight by five feet. From where she stood she could see several tall racks, containing hundreds of bottles of wine turned on their sides, each resting in its own curved slot.

She heard a rustle behind the first rack and saw the movement of a shadow. She froze, clutching the bottles before her like a shield. "Who—who's there?" she called, knowing that there weren't really any "deranged" Hunts around, but not quite convinced of her safety.

"What?" A silver head appeared from around the side of the rack. Cotter looked almost as surprised to see her as she was to see him. With a curious frown, he came out and leaned against the end of the rack, scanning her burden. "What are you doing with those?"

"Nordie—"

Her explanation was jarred out of her mind with the loud slam of the door at their backs. Startled by the unexpected explosion of sound, she let go of the bottles, and they crashed to the cement floor, popping and shattering around her sandaled feet.

Openmouthed, she stared down at the mess. "Oh, no!"

"Ooooh, noooo!" She heard her words repeated at her back, but it was less of an echo and more like a banshee's wail. She spun around to see Nordie's face pinched between the center bars. Her hands were curled around the outer two. She was looking in forlornly at them, her expression one of total distress. "I—I hate to say this, folks. But I think the door's locked."

Chapter Ten

"Locked?" Raine questioned, feeling vaguely uneasy.

"Nordie." Cotter walked forward, past Raine, his shoes crunching glass as he moved to the door. "This isn't funny. Open up."

She regarded him soberly. "Cot, I'm not kidding. I was on my way down with the last two empty bottles when the wind just blew it shut. And that big lock slid in with the force." She moved her hands down to curl around the thick pine window frame. "You know how rusty the sea air can make things. I'm afraid it's stuck."

"Nordie, there's no wind down here," he growled, lowering his voice so that she had to strain to hear him.

"Well, of course there is—I mean with the patio doors open, and the front door, and the kitchen. It was a freak wind." Nordie screwed up her face in a puzzled frown. "What is it they have at airports?"

Another Man's Treasure   181

"For God's sake, Nordie, open this door."

"I'm trying to explain, Cotter." She looked put out. "What do they have...at airports?"

"Hell, I don't know. What? Moonies? Insurance machines? Who cares!"

"Well, I do! I mean those dangerous, big winds— you know."

"What dangerous, big winds? Campaigning politicians?"

Raine bit her upper lip to keep from smiling. She didn't know why Cotter's exasperated tone was funny, but somehow it was. Apparently Nordie thought so, too. She burst out laughing. "No, wind sheets...shorts. Oh, I don't know."

"Shears. Wind shears." Raine helped.

"Right!" Nordie held up a finger. "Anyway, Cotter. It was probably a wind shear. Or even a convection current." She lifted her chin and offered her brother a superior smile. "I bet you didn't think I learned anything when I dated that meteorology student."

"Nordie!" Cotter's hands went up to the bars, and Nordie immediately stepped away from the window. "I hope you own plenty of black clothes—to wear in memory of your dear, departed sanity! Now open this damn door or, I swear, this time..." He let his words fade and then proceeded to whisper to her. Raine tried to hear but couldn't.

"Maybe one of the boys could help?" Raine suggested.

"Aw, darn," Nordie intoned sadly, "they insisted on going with Carl and Cammie to help move some of the heavier stuff in. But they'll be back in three or four hours—maybe five."

Cotter rattled the bars menacingly. Raine couldn't see Nordie from her vantage point and wondered if she was intimidated by Cotter. She decided to intervene in her behalf. "Really, Cotter, you can't blame the girl. Another minute and she'd have been trapped in here with us."

Cotter peered at Raine over one shoulder, taking in her slender form with a pitying gaze. "You think so?"

She nodded. "Why, of course."

He smiled wanly and shook his head in wry amusement before he turned his attention back to his sister. "Okay, Nordie. Then go get Ike Noonan."

"Ike?" She said the name as though she'd completely forgotten his existence.

"Yes, you know—the 'hunk.'"

"Ooh! Ike. Uh, I..." Her voice faltered, and she paused for a moment. "Okay, I'll go look for him."

"Nordie," Cotter warned, "try to look in places he might be."

"I sure will. What do you take me for?" Her giggle grew dim. And Raine could hear her brisk footsteps disappear up the steps.

Cotter turned away from the window and leaned heavily against the door. He was silent, apparently deep in thought, his eyes on the broken glass between them.

The silence loomed. Raine decided to speak first. "There wouldn't be a broom in here, would there?"

Cotter looked up. "A broom?"

She spread her hands. "For the glass. I thought we could sweep it into a pile."

He shook his head, stepping over it. "No." He took her elbow. "There are some cases of wine against the wall back here. While we're waiting, why don't we sit? We could even have a drink."

"No...thanks." She removed her elbow from his grasp, deciding that it would be better to keep busy, keep moving. "I'll find a piece of cardboard or something and get this glass in a pile. You go ahead and sit."

He crossed his arms and gazed thoughtfully at her. "You know, you're going to have to stop throwing yourself at me like this, or people will start to talk."

The vaguely belligerent remark took her so by surprise, her lips parted in a stunned "oh." After a few seconds, he answered her silence with a long exhalation. "Don't panic, professor. I was being sarcastic." He took her arm again and led her toward the back where four wooden crates were stacked, two on two. He suggested quietly, "Why don't we just sit down and wait to be rescued."

There was a patchwork quilt folded neatly on top of one. "Hmm." He cocked his head to one side, staring at it.

"What?" She asked following his gaze.

"That quilt doesn't belong here." He stuck it under one arm as he lifted the top two boxes off. Putting the folded blanket on top of one of the crates, he swept an arm toward it. "But as long as it is..." Though he smiled in invitation for her to sit, he seemed edgy, preoccupied.

She felt uneasy but sat down.

He startled her by settling on the crate beside her. They were so close, she had to draw away to keep their arms from brushing. Agitated, she closed her hands in a tight ball in her lap. Just then all the lights went off, leaving them in complete darkness. Raine gasped.

Cotter groaned deep in his throat. "Cover your ears," he said. "I'm going to get my sister's attention." He sat forward and she thought she could see him cup his hands at his mouth. "Nora Diane Hunt! Raine will have you brought up on charges of kidnapping if you don't cut this out right now."

They listened to the silence long enough to know that there would be no answer. Raine whispered, "Why do you believe Nordie is behind this?"

Cotter's chuckle held no humor. "Just a wild hunch."

"I can't imagine why you'd think such a thing. What could she possibly hope to gain by trapping us in the wine cellar?"

He sat back against the wall. "I've given up on trying to understand her. Maybe she's practicing on us for a bigger caper. Or even more insidious, maybe she wants us to be alone together so that we can make amends." He sounded totally disgusted.

Raine caught her breath. His malevolent tone hurt. She stammered, "Why—why would she do that?"

"Which?"

She felt provoked and managed to whisper, "You know which."

His big shoulders, clothed in white, lifted in a shrug. Looking up, she thought she could make out his features now. His eyes, though dark, were gleaming. And she could tell that he was watching her closely. "She'd like to have you in the family. It's painfully obvious we need more brains."

Raine's pride was hurt by his continued sarcasm. She countered churlishly, "Maybe you'd better tell her brains aren't what you want in a woman."

"Hey!" Nordie called from far away. "What's with the lights? It's dark all over the house."

"I wouldn't know, Nordie. I'm trapped in the wine cellar, remember?" Cotter called crossly. "Have you found Ike?"

"No. He didn't answer when I knocked on his door. I figure he's either out patrolling the grounds—

like a typical cop, never around when you need him—or else he's passed out in a drunken stupor somewhere."

"Oh, good." Cotter didn't sound at all pleased. "Well, you do your best. And when I get out of here I'll reward you."

"My very plan, Cot," she shouted. "Say, I have an idea. Why don't I drive into Portland and help unload Carl and Cam, and then bring the guys back. Together I bet we can get you two out."

Cotter bolted to his feet. "Don't leave this house, Nordie Hunt! Nordie?"

When the echoes of his sister's name died away, it was so quiet Raine could hear Cotter gritting his teeth.

"Damn!" he muttered, sitting down again. "It'll be hours now."

It was obvious that he didn't relish the idea of being left alone with her. Her fingers tightened in her lap. "Don't mind me," she bit out. "I won't bother you."

He turned to face her. "Actually, I was thinking of you."

She laughed shortly. "Your sarcasm is getting a little thin.

"I mean it, Raine," he admitted more softly. "I'm really sorry about this prank."

Her hands were becoming sweaty, and she unclasped them, rubbing them on her legs. "You don't really expect me to believe Nordie did this on purpose?

"No? And, why did you bring those empty bottles down here?" he probed.

"I don't know. Nordie asked me to. She'd hurt her ankle—"

"Her ankle?" he interjected, incredulously. "She recovered mighty fast, then." Raine frowned in thought as he went on. "Of course, I could be wrong. I don't have the education you have. Maybe wind shears in basements are fairly common."

She pushed her glasses more securely on her nose and peered over at his face. She couldn't see his features very clearly, just his eyes. They seemed to be narrowed. She couldn't tell if the expression was one of anger or skepticism.

Maybe—maybe he was right. Maybe Nordie actually had done it. If she had, it was a childish thing to do. Terribly embarrassing for both her and Cotter. He didn't want to be here any more than she did. Clearing her throat, she returned her hands to her lap, not quite knowing what to say.

They sat for a long time in silence before Raine was startled by a wry chuckle. "Say," Cotter suggested glibly, covering Raine's hands with his own, "when she gets back, let's tell her we're engaged. I'd love to see her face."

The unexpected touch was warming against her icy fingers. She hadn't realized how cold she was until he touched her. Feeling annoyed, she jerked away and jumped to her feet. If he was going for shock value, he would appreciate her sudden response. Angrily, she hissed, "Why must you forever be conniving? If you want to know the truth, Cotter, I blame you, and you alone, for this!" She backed into a wine rack, bracing her arms out at her sides, whispering harshly, "Who could really blame Nordie for this? After all, monkey see, monkey do!"

His shadowy features closed in a grimace as he slowly stood up. "Damn it all!" he raged. One step brought him directly in front of her, and only inches away. "I wish I could make you understand—about everything—but I told you once, I can't."

"No," she corrected with a proud lift of her chin, "You told me once, you won't. I don't want to—to talk."

"Fine." He covered her white-knuckled hands, adding, "Then we won't." To her utter astonishment, he pressed himself boldly against her. "We get along much better when we don't." His voice had become a husky whisper, taking on a strange finality.

As he lowered his face to hers she felt as if she were in a dream. Her lips were poised and invitingly opened. His hands moved up her arms until they were entwining around her back, one moving up to caress the nape of her neck softly, the other, down, covering the curve of one soft hip.

"I wish..." she whispered in a breathless voice, unable to finish, to actually say the words. She wished they possessed what each of them was looking for. But they didn't. Nevertheless, she was slipping into the hopeless tangle of his arms. Knowing their satisfaction would be only temporary, she fought against her building passion, forcing her eyes to flutter open. With an effort born of desperation, she spread her hands against his hard chest, pushing, to remind him of their differences. "I—I'm nothing...you want...."

"Don't." He groaned, lowering his lips to her throat, eager to show her tenderness. The muttered word became a plea.

A slight tug at the top button of her blouse, and her thin barrier against him began to fall silently away. She sighed against the warm pressure of his searching touch as his hands moved to the other buttons and slipped off her blouse, exposing her to the tingling caress of his tongue.

Dropping to his knees, he deftly removed her glasses and held her to him. His silver hair felt thick and soft against her fingers as she gently stroked the head that suckled and teased her yielding softness.

A quiet cry carried his name as they parted briefly. And then, quickly, he was lifting her into his arms, placing her on the surprisingly soft quilt, which protected her from the cold cement floor.

She lifted her hands to his shirt, astonished at how surely and swiftly her fingers parted the cloth. In a concert of movement, they relieved each other of the rest of their clothes and joined completely. With a long, dreamy sigh, she knew again the length and breadth of their mutual need. She curled her arms about the quaking muscles of his back as he led her farther into the swirling sea of their lovemaking.

He turned slightly, and she found herself riding the crest of their seething sea, rising and dipping, tossed along on their own tactile ocean. On waves of pleasure she rode, her head high, as she reveled in the storm, drenched and glistening.

Crying out, she shuddered her delight, and as she did, she felt his large hands come up and press her softness down to his chest. His lips against her forehead kissed and nipped lightly at hers. They lay entwined, breathing heavily, their hearts pounding like surf on the rocks in the aftermath of a storm. But the memory of their union lingered in the sweet, wet tingling of their bodies.

She glowed, then cooled, shivering in his arms. He held tightly to her as he turned her slightly, covering her body with his. "Better?" His low whisper was hoarse with desire.

She ran a hand along his back. It felt solid and slick. Nodding, she turned her face away. But the lump in her throat would not allow her to speak. She loved this man and knew he could inflame her. At this moment, she refused to let thoughts of their differences invade her mind. This was something she would accept as a singular experience.

She held tightly to him, wondering if he'd found what he was looking for in any other woman. Had women always flocked to Cotter? It was a discouraging thought. He lifted a hand to her jaw, turning her face up to his. She couldn't avoid looking into his dark, glistening eyes. "We must be out of our minds," he muttered against her cheek before lightly kissing her there. "Any minute now Nordie and her entourage could come back and the world would know about this. They'd never allow us to forget it."

Never allow us to forget it! She closed her eyes and tried to push the thought away. But there it was in a nutshell. Their lovemaking was something to be forgotten, not a symbol of a deep emotion.

As her arms dropped listlessly from his back, she murmured sadly, "Yes, we shouldn't be forced to remember."

"Hmm?" He turned his head slightly, kissing her cheek—wet with tears. Lifting his head, he licked the moisture from his lips and peered down at her. "Talk to me now, Raine."

She had told Cotter once that she hated fighting, and it was true. But she hated being used, deplored the emptiness of their act. Cotter seemed to have no idea what was wrong. He had no inkling that she had not been able to deny him because she loved him. He didn't understand what it was to love someone hopelessly. He only understood how to use her.

Anger and hurt flared inside her. Licking dry lips, she began what she knew would be difficult to say. "Please go away, Cotter." The voice she heard coming from her own lips was so low, so determined, she didn't recognize it.

He lay still, saying nothing, not moving. She pressed the damp cheek down to the quilt and inhaled a calming breath, wishing she could know what was going through his mind just then. It couldn't be shame that was motivating him now. She had made love with him a second time without reciprocal love or hope. Negating her weakness, she repeated her demand, her voice growing stronger with conviction. "I said, please go."

When he rolled away, she sat up, hugging herself, feeling weak and bereft. He sat up as well, drawing himself up beside her.

"Cotter..." she pleaded, turning to face him squarely. "A long time ago, my father told me never to use the word 'hate.' But I'm going to break that rule. You've lied to me from the moment we met. I hate you for that!"

He had picked up her shirt and held it out to her when she'd begun to speak. Now he was very still. She took the shirt from his outstretched hand and swept her underwear and slacks up as she moved away from him. Hurrying to the far corner to put on her clothes, she worked at keeping her voice calm, "You said once that I was too nice. Maybe not anymore. I'm not dumb, Cotter—I'm learning. I can even make up rules of my own. You want to hear one?" She jerked on her underwear, whispering hoarsely, "Don't touch me anymore. That's my only rule, the only one I need. You can find somebody else to play your games with."

"But Raine—" He had followed her, and his fingers curled around her bare shoulder, but she jerked away, struggling into her shirt.

"Go away, please. I asked you not to touch me!"

"But you can't—"

"Hey, down there! We're back! Anybody care?" The familiar singsong voice, calling from far away, commanded their attention. Raine's gasp was audible, and she hurried to finish dressing.

Cotter muttered something and Raine could hear the rustle of his clothes being pulled hurriedly on as he shouted back, "That five hours breezed right by!" He made no attempt to hide the irritation in his voice.

"We could go out and bring back a couple of pizzas. You two like anchovies?" Nordie's voice was as light as Cotter's had been grave.

Raine smoothed her hair back with trembling fingers and adjusted her glasses as she turned to look at Cotter. She was startled to see his dark eyes glittering as he called sardonically, "Don't bother. I don't think Professor Webber is hungry. Get your friends down here and open this door."

The lights came on, and Raine dropped her gaze from Cotter's face. With an urgent need to have the whole incident blotted from her brain, she pushed by him and busied herself by gathering the quilt into her arms, fumbling to get it folded.

Cotter took it from her and made quick work of folding it, placing it on top of the crate she'd been sitting on earlier. As he straightened, Nordie came to the door.

"Well, there's what comes from having brains in the group. George just flicked something he called a breaker and presto! Lights."

Cotter walked forward a pace. "You mean you didn't try that yourself?"

She grinned. "I'm no electrical engineer."

"Not this semester, anyway," Cotter said simply. "Give George my thanks. But a prison with lights is still a prison." His tone was matter-of-fact now, all irritation gone or well hidden. Most likely, Raine thought, she was already forgotten. He was speaking. "How do you intend to get that lock un—"

A noisy scraping and then a loud thud cut off his words, and the door opened. Nordie beamed at them, stepping back. *"Voilà"* She took a bow as though she were being wildly applauded. Holding up her hands, palms forward, she shook her head.

"Thank you! Thank you! But it was nothing—nothing at all."

In a surprise move, Cotter took Raine's elbow in a grasp so firm she doubted that she could disengage him without throwing herself to the floor. He helped her step over the glass while speaking to Nordie, "For your sake, I hope you didn't do that by yourself."

She laughed, pulling Bill out from behind the door. "Of course not. My hero did it. I've always been partial to brawny, earthy-type men. That's why I love you so much. You can't get much earthier than a garbageman." She threw her brother a kiss, then sobered until only the merest glint of devilment remained in her eyes. "I sure hope you two weren't too inconvenienced being stuck in there like that. But at least it didn't take as long as I thought it would to get you out. Carl sent the boys back. I met them on the road. Seems Carl told them he and Cam were tired and wanted to go on to bed."

With Cotter's hand on her arm, Raine had trouble concentrating on the conversation. Why was he doing this to her? Was it part of his perverse sense of humor? Was he doing it because she'd asked him not to touch her again? Probably. She despised being manipulated and made a fool of. Her cheeks grew hot with anger. With an abrupt step forward she jerked away from him, using all her might. "I'm going to bed. Tomorrow's a workday, and I don't feel very well," she muttered between clenched teeth.

"You don't?" Nordie asked, sounding surprised.

"Oh, it's been a long day, I guess." She knew her face was tight, her voice strained. But Nordie could take it—she couldn't always see Raine as a paragon. "Good night, Nordie, Bill." When she rounded the door, she almost ran headlong into George. "Oh!" She dropped her hands to his shoulders. "I didn't know you were there. Thanks for your help, George."

His face reddened in his shy, embarrassed way. "It's okay," he mumbled, stepping out of her way.

Even feeling as desolate as she did, her heart went out to him. She knew how he felt. She'd been as painfully shy at his age, too. Patting his arm affectionately, she headed past him. Her trammeled heart pounded in rhythm with her feet as she retreated, in a near run, up the steps, toward the sanctity of her room.

Nordie, a perplexed expression knitting her fine brows, watched Raine go. She then turned to the young men. "You guys go on up to bed. Cotter and I have some family stuff to discuss. You know, stuff like who's going to cook breakfast, and who's the beneficiary of his estate...."

When they had gone, Nordie turned a jaundiced eye on her brother. She began to tap one foot. "Do you see that?" She cocked her head down toward the thumping high heel.

"Is that the sprained ankle?"

"Don't try to change the subject," she warned glumly. "No, it's intense irritation. She looked angrier than ever. What did you do in there?"

He crossed his arms and stared at her. "You amaze me. Just what did you expect me to do once you got us trapped in there?"

Nordie threw up her hands in exaggerated distress. "I expected you to do what you usually do."

He frowned at her. "I usually get wine."

She matched his look and poked him in the ribs. "I didn't mean that! Didn't you take the golden opportunity in there in the dark to tell her how much you like her?"

"Are you still on that?" he hedged, looking away, searching the dusky corners of the basement for something—preferably an escape route. His sister's probing was making him feel like a bum.

"Why shouldn't I be? I planned this little prank to give you some time alone with her to—to plight your troth—without that handsome cop hanging around. What did you two do, argue politics? If you did, from the way she looked when she left, I'd wager you two would never have met at a political convention."

"We didn't talk much." He sighed heavily. "And I told you once, I'm not 'plighting' anything to any woman. I have enough family to worry about with you and Carl." He turned back to face her. "This trick of yours was a fine idea. She couldn't abide me before; now she has a healthy hatred for me." He lifted a fist threateningly to her chin. "And you know whose fault that is."

"Oh, really?" She pushed his hand away. "When Professor Webber looked at me just now, her eyes didn't say she wished *I* were covered with honey in a cage full of hungry bears." She slid him a sly glance. "Besides, I can no more make women hate you than I can make 'em love you. If you didn't tell her you liked her, just what did you do to that sweet woman?"

He knew what he'd done. And he knew it hadn't been a fair thing to do—especially twice. He didn't know what it was about Raine that attracted him so deeply. But whatever it was, it could short-circuit his common sense. He leaned back against the cold brick wall. There was something undeniable about her; something vital, yet fragile, that made her lovable.

Nordie squinted up at Cotter's face. "Why you—" her voice had become high-pitched and disbelieving "—Why you lecher! I can see guilt all over your face! You tried to take advantage of her down here. You rat! You weren't supposed to do that; you were supposed to talk nice to her! Can't you tell a lady when you see one? Are you nothing but an animal?" She accented her scolding words by punching his stomach.

"Ouch! Cut it out, Nordie." He held out his hand to ward off further attack.

"And you try to say it's my fault? After all, I set this thing up! I wanted to be Cupid and I turned out to be a—an accessory! I can't believe it! My own brother!" Ignoring his grunt of pain, she jabbed a finger toward the stairs. "Get out of here. I never want to see you again."

He looked at her seriously now. "Are you quite through, Your Majesty?"

She swiveled her head slowly around. "Are you still here, you worm?"

"Okay, okay." he grumbled, running a hand through his hair. "I admit I'm all manner of crawling lowlife—probably worse. But I haven't gotten off unscathed. Between the two of you, I'm getting my share of bruises."

"Aw! What a bummer for you." She lifted her lips in a satisfied smile. "Therein lies the message."

He reached up to rub his throbbing temples. "Look, I'm already in pain. What do you expect me to do? Throw myself off a cliff?"

"Why don't you?" She lifted a shoulder in a dismissing shrug. "Professor Webber will be gone in a few days anyway—probably be engaged to Ike by then. I suppose that's for the best." She sighed theatrically. "Meanwhile, why don't you give Anona a call. She doesn't have the sense to hate you." She didn't wait for an answer, but spun away and stomped up the steps.

Cotter said nothing. Maybe Anona had the sense to now. He hadn't said anything specific to her tonight. But she knew he wasn't going to call her anymore. He'd seen it in her eyes after he'd kissed her good-bye. Anona knew the rules.

He turned away from the empty stairs as his sister's steps echoed a staccato retreat through the kitchen. His eyes were drawn back into the wine cellar; his brooding gaze fell on the folded quilt. The memory of Raine's yielding body blazed to life again, and his mouth tightened. He didn't need complications in his life. Things were exactly the way he wanted them to be, or they would be soon.

Raine was leaving in a few days, and with her gone, Nordie's fickle anger would abate. All he had to do was wait both women out. It was that simple. Feeling drained, he leaned a shoulder against the doorjamb and closed his eyes. If it was so simple, then why did he feel so damned bad?

Chapter Eleven

Raine flinched when the stable door creaked open, fearing it might be Cotter. Fumbling with the cola bottle she had been cataloguing, she allowed it to tumble off the table and onto the hay-strewn ground. She leaned against the table for strength. She had managed to avoid seeing him at breakfast by skipping the meal. She hoped that had made her position clear enough. Surely he wouldn't have the audacity to come out here where he knew she would be, not after last night. She hoped he'd have the decency, at least, to go to his office in town these last few days.

"Morning, everybody. Sorry I'm late."

Raine breathed a sigh of relief and turned around. Her smile was more a show of teeth than an emotional reaction to Ike. But she had to admit, she much preferred seeing Ike Noonan than Cotter Hunt. "Hi. You oversleep?" She managed the question in a normal tone of voice.

He nodded sheepishly. "Yeah. I forgot to set the alarm. Did I miss anything?"

Nordie chimed in, "Did you ever! Last night Professor Webber and my—" her eyes darted fleetingly, almost apologetically, to Raine and back again to Ike "—my brother got trapped in the wine cellar. Nobody was here to help me get them out. At least, everybody else was gone. And I couldn't find you." She paused.

Ike's expression closed. "Really? When?"

"Oh, I guess it was about twenty minutes or so after everybody left."

Ike rubbed his jaw thoughtfully as he considered that. "I was in my room. Guess I was in the shower. Went right to bed. Never heard a thing."

Nordie smacked her forehead with the palm of her hand, declaring loudly, "Of course! In the shower. I should have guessed that. And if you went right off to bed, you probably didn't even know the electricity went off."

"It did?" Ike appeared totally surprised. Letting out a hearty laugh, he quipped, "And I'm supposed to be a detective?"

Nordie giggled. "It was off for about an hour. I wish you'd have seen me trying to get out through our gate without electricity. Manual operation of that electronic thing is the pits."

"I'm sorry." Ike walked over to the hook that held his smock. "But since Raine is standing here, I gather everything came out all right."

Nordie folded her rubber-gloved hands and looked over at Raine. "Well—" she smiled weakly and shrugged "—everybody escaped, if that's what you mean."

Ike pulled his smock on and began buttoning it. "Good." He ambled over to Raine. "You got anything for me yet?"

She shook her head, handing him a pair of gloves. "No. I was just about to get started on our special bags." She picked up the wire cutters and broke the identifying seal. "Your timing was perfect." He grinned and winked.

An hour passed. Raine and Ike had just opened the second bag in the suspect group when Raine pulled out a crumpled sheet of pink paper. She repeated the code for writing paper as she carefully smoothed it out. "It's a letter—at least part of one. It's been burned." She scanned the contents, taking care not to break off any of the blackened edges where writing could still be made out. "Want to take a look at it?"

His back was toward her. She heard him wad a charge-card receipt he had been carefully examining. "Sure. If nothing else, it'll be a break in the monotony." He tossed the crumpled receipt in the catalogued trash. "May be from a lover."

She scanned the flowing script. "It does look like a woman's handwriting. But if it's a love letter, it's pretty tame. Something about grapes—" as she skimmed the words, she held the paper out to him "—and some friend that went fishing."

His fingers froze an inch from the fragile page, and his eyes grew wide. For a long moment, he stared down at it.

"What is it?" She looked from his face back to the letter and frowned in confusion. Certainly there was nothing in the partial note that looked incriminating.

"Give me that," he murmured. Snatching the sheet from her, he pored over it closely. His fingers began to tremble as he read aloud. "Cousin...grapes we've sown will make good wine. Our friend's gone fishing. Paulie—" Ike's voice caught oddly. Swallowing, he began again. "Paulie's gone to the...country."

Raine looked up at his face. He had gone pale. In a whisper, she asked, "How do you know it's 'country'? All it says is 'Paulie's gone to the co.' It could be company or—"

He looked up from the paper, crumpling it in his fist. Raine grimaced at his unprofessional treatment of what appeared to be important evidence. She was about to caution him about it when he said in a low voice, "It's 'country.'"

He stared at nothing in particular and was so silent for so long, Raine finally had to touch his arm to get his attention.

"Ike? What's wrong?"

He jerked his head around to meet her concerned look. His lips turned up in a woeful smile, and his eyes were vacant. "Nothing," he mumbled shortly, clutching the letter like a hand grenade about to explode. "I've got my evidence." He looked at her face for only an instant, and his features hardened. "It's just not...what I expected. Thought it'd be a phone number, an airline charge, something on a credit card, but not—" Licking his lips, he seemed to have an idea. "Look. Where's a paper? I need to see a newspaper."

Glancing around, Raine nodded. "We've catalogued several of this morning's." Before she could go on, Ike was already thumbing through a rumpled copy. He dropped to his knees, spreading the sections out on the dirt floor. Raine sat beside him. "What is it, Ike? May I help?"

He shook his head as he scanned page after page. Raine looked around, realizing her students had stopped what they were doing and stood staring. She didn't blame them. Ike was acting strangely. When she had turned back, Ike was crouched over a small article, his finger moving slowly as he read.

She squinted to see what had attracted his attention. The headline said: "Hit Man's Body Discovered." The story originated in San Clemente, California. She had only a moment to see that it had something to do with the recent murder of Joseph DeMosso, the alleged head of one of the largest crime families operating out of Los Angeles. The body, the story went on to say, had been identified as that of Rocky Velasquez, an alleged hit man. It had been discovered by swimmers after it had washed up on a local beach.

Ike slammed the paper down and jumped to his feet, cursing under his breath. "Why—why Doria?"

Raine scrambled up after him, asking fearfully, "What is it, Ike? Who is Doria?"

He had already pulled off his smock and spun around, his eyes as hard and cutting as steel. "Nothing. Forget it." He stuffed the page into his suit coat pocket. "I'd better get this...to my boss."

Raine didn't appreciate his mysteriousness. He was taking the letter too personally and withholding information from her. She caught his arm as he headed toward the door. "Ike, I'm going, too. You'll need corroboration, won't you? After all, I found the letter." She wanted to say what she really felt, that there was something about him that didn't ring true. And she was not about to let him leave without knowing what it was.

He stopped short at her touch, staring down at her as though he'd never seen her before. "No, uh, no." He spoke as if in a daze.

Nordie dashed between them and clutched each of them by an arm. Her eyes were bright with excitement. "Oh, Ike! But Professor Webber uncovered the evidence. Surely they'll want to talk to her! This is so exciting! Let me go, too. Let's all go. We're eyewitnesses." She beamed. "Imagine. We might even get to testify." Turning back to Ike, she said, "Ike, we will get to testify, won't we?"

His steely gaze narrowed. "I'll send someone by later to get your statements. Nobody goes with me now."

Raine felt a shiver of apprehension at the guarded undertone in his voice. For some reason, she was frightened of him—and for him. It occurred to her that he might be thinking of suppressing the evidence. Maybe a fellow officer had been implicated by the letter. It was obvious that something was very different from what he'd expected. By accompanying him, she could perhaps prevent him from doing something rash—something that would get him in terrible trouble with the department. Pulling off her gloves and smock, she declared, "I'm going with you, of course. I found the letter, and I intend to see this through."

A muscle jerked in his cheek, betraying a strong irritation, but Raine stood firm, matching his stare with one of equal determination.

She was surprised when at last he nodded. "You choose now to become assertive, professor? Your timing could have been better. Let's go, then. But I wish it could have been otherwise." Turning to Nordie, he took her hand, uncurling her arm from his. "Good-bye, Miss Hunt. Tell your brother that your professor insisted."

He cocked his head toward Raine but his eyes did not quite meet hers. He hurried her from the stables. What did he mean, "Tell your brother that your professor insisted"? What did Cotter have to do with this? Why would he care if she went to the police station? Strange, inconsistent behavior.

They'd traveled silently for several miles when Raine asked, "Ike? How does the letter figure in with the crime you're investigating?"

He was watching the road, his knuckles white in a tight grip on the steering wheel. His frown deepened, and with a swiftness that made her grab for her balance, he turned off into a secluded, wooded lane.

Dust rose around them as he braked the car and turned to face her, his features hard and sad.

"What," she asked, "are you doing?"

He reached inside his suit coat and drew out a gun, leveling it at her. She stared down at it in disbelief. Her lips fell open, and she could do nothing but watch the weapon as it was moved slowly toward her.

"I'm sorry, Raine. I don't want to do this. But because of your determination, I didn't have a choice." The metal felt cold as it touched her ribs.

With a tremendous effort, she managed to pull her eyes from the gun and focus on Ike's face. There was an ironic look of pity in his eyes. Her mouth worked soundlessly, forming the word "Why?"

He responded immediately. "Because you read the letter."

"The letter?" she breathed. "But it didn't say anything..."

He smiled sadly. "To you. But you saw the words. Others would understand."

"What?" She winced as the gun began to bruise her flesh. "Please..." Her voice trembled as her mind tried to grasp reality. She couldn't believe this man actually intended to kill her. Someone would come along....

She had to keep him talking for a few minutes. Swallowing to ease the fear blocking her throat, she fought for a reprieve with her only weapon, logic. "Please, Ike, tell me what the letter means. If you're going to kill me, at least let me know why."

Cocking his head, he motioned for her to open the door. "Move very slowly and don't make any rash moves. I want to get my business done and leave all this."

Her palms sweated and her hands trembled so much that she could barely open the door. She got out of the car and stood up on watery legs. Ike slid across the seat, keeping the gun pressed firmly against her ribs. "You're gonna ride in the trunk for a while. I can't have anybody finding your—you until I give cousin Eddy a little present."

She swallowed, staring straight ahead and listening intently for the crunch of tires along the road, but the only sound she could hear was the wind rustling the highest branches of the pines. He poked her again in the ribs. "Lie down on your stomach."

She got down on the ground, turning her face to the side. He pulled her hands to her back, binding them with his tie. She asked him as calmly as she could, "Who...is this cousin?"

He took one final tug on her hands, and she cried out in pain. His answer came while he moved to her feet. "Eddy conspired to murder my father, Joseph DeMosso."

Raine was stunned and twisted around to try to see him. He had removed his belt and was working it around her knees. "Your...father?"

He looked up. "I'm Paul DeMosso."

"Paulie..." She said the word out loud before she realized she had said anything. Still in an awed murmur, she repeated what she remembered from the letter. "Paulie's gone to the country...."

His grin was melancholy. "Yeah. Means I'm in hiding, just in case whoever got Joseph was after me, too. The king is dead. Long live the king. If I'd only known," he mumbled, yanking the belt tight. "Ed Fusco—the cousin mentioned in the letter—he's family. Handles drug trafficking from here. Always been a greedy guy, but he's family. When Joseph got hit, I had a feeling it was Eddy but, being family, I needed proof before I took him out. Today, I got it."

She heard the trunk pop open, and stiffened, knowing she was about to be imprisoned in its cramped darkness. Why didn't a car come? Why didn't somebody—anybody—come? She felt herself being lifted, and gasped out of sheer desperation. "But—but wait! Who wrote the letter? Who conspired with—"

"Quiet!" he snapped, carrying her as though she were no weight at all. More carefully than she expected, he laid her down on her side. She watched as he took a linen handkerchief from his pocket and folded it like a gag. "So," he went on, biting out every word, "like I said, when my father was hit, I had a gut feeling it was Ed's doing—had his style. Sure enough, that Velasquez they found on the beach is a Florida boy Ed's used before." He laughed bitterly as he tied the gag about Raine's mouth. "Looks like old Ed got his—" he grimaced, spitting out the word "—partner to get rid of Velasquez. Too big a hit to leave witnesses. Like the letter said, their friend went fishing."

Her eyes grew wide, but she couldn't speak because of the gag, and she coughed at the dryness of the cloth against her tongue.

He sighed, looking past her. "But the real reason you have to die is because of who Ed conspired with." He put his hands on the trunk lid, and Raine knew that very soon she would be trapped in darkness. She stared at his face, and was shocked to see his eyes cloud with tears. "Doria." He shook his head. "Ed's Doria's cousin, not mine. I knew Doria was ambitious for me to take over. But I never thought my own wife would conspire to kill my father. Damn it! I love that woman. She's the mother of my kids. Don't you see? I can't let anyone live who knows she was in on it."

Raine blinked up at him, stunned at what he was saying. He was going to kill this Ed Fusco, but he was going to keep his wife's part in the murder a secret. He was going to kill her to protect his wife from sure revenge at the hands of those loyal to Joseph, men who wouldn't spare her just because she was the wife of Paul DeMosso.

His low chuckle was dry and bitter. "I see you understand that I've got to trade your life for Doria's." He reached down and traced her cheek with a finger, and she drew away. He smiled his understanding. "I like you. Your death will haunt me. I'm sorry."

The world went black for Raine, but she continued to stare at the place she had last seen Ike's face—or Paul DeMosso's face. The anguished determination that had glittered in his eyes made her numb with fear. She was going to die because he loved a woman so much that he was willing to kill and kill again to keep her deadly secret. And she would die, never having known love at all.

WHEN NORDIE BARGED through the doors of Cotter's den, he glanced at her with little interest. He had been staring at nothing in particular, his chin on his fists. Their eyes met only for an instant before he looked away, to stare again at nothing. The strains of "Round about Midnight" laced his thoughts with melancholy memories of the last time he'd heard it. With Raine. His eyes slid to the couch, and he could see her there again, so trusting—so caring and vulnerable.

"Well!" Nordie thrust her chin high. "I heard the music, or I'd never have guessed you'd slithered back home."

He shifted an unbrothered gaze back to her. "Good afternoon to you, too."

She marched over and took the needle off the record. "I'm not speaking to you, remember. But I think you should hear this."

He sat back, asking, "Do I have a vote?"

"Oh, be quiet! This is important." She couldn't stifle her smile completely in her enthusiasm to tell him the good news. "We've solved the crime!" With a laugh and a thumbs-up, she walked to his desk, leaning toward him. "Professor Webber and Ike Noonan left a good twenty minutes ago to take our evidence to headquarters. Isn't that exciting?"

He was surprised. "Oh?" Crossing his arms before him, he inquired calmly, "What did they find?"

She shrugged, stepping back. "Don't know."

He mocked her, "*We've* solved the crime, and *we* don't know what *our* evidence was? Congratulations, Charlie Chan."

She tossed her head. "You'll be laughing on the other side of that face when *we* get *our* names in the paper and *you* don't!" Without waiting for a response, she went on, her excitement animating her face, "But listen, Cotter, whatever the evidence was, it made Ike real excited, almost—" she frowned, tapping a finger on her nose in thought "—almost angry." She waved that thought away. "No, not angry, really. More like...crazed. Crazed and wired. I'm dying to know what they found."

Cotter became lost in thought. "That's an odd way for a cop to react to finding evidence he's been after for two weeks. You must have misinterpreted."

"Me?" She sniffed derisively. "Once again, you underestimate my powers of observation. But I won't argue the point now. Ike wanted me to give you a message. I admit that I didn't get it. But I quote: 'Tell your brother—'" she cocked her head toward him "'—that your professor insisted.'"

He lifted a puzzled brow. "Insisted? On what?"

She shook her head. "I don't know. Going with him, I guess. He didn't want her to. He didn't want anybody to go."

Cotter frowned, feeling uneasy but acutely interested. "I don't understand. You'd think—"

A soft rapping at the door drew their attention. Cotter called out, "Come in."

"Sir?" Hanna pushed the door ajar and slipped inside. "There's a Detective Hefflet here to see you." Dropping her voice, she added, "From the police."

Cotter exchanged curious glances with his sister before he said, "Please have him come in, Hanna."

She slipped out as quietly as she had entered, and after a brief moment, a balding, rather bony man about Cotter's age entered, closing the door behind him. He was dressed in a black suit that give him a somber look. With a smile that was all business, he stepped forward to take Cotter's hand. "How do you do, Mr. Hunt? I'm Detective Ray Hefflet." After a perfunctory handshake, he produced his identification. "I was hoping you and your people could help me."

Nordie clasped her hands together delightedly. "Oh, good. You want us to testify! I just knew it!"

Detective Hefflet turned toward her, his expression registering slight curiosity. Cotter lifted a hand in his sister's direction. "Ray, this is my sister, Nordie. And I'm Cotter. How may we help?"

Detective Hefflet explained, "We are aware that a group of university students have been doing a study of garbage at some Portland residences with the help of your service."

Cotter nodded, but his frown returned. Why was this man reiterating something that was news as old to both him and the police department as last month's garbage? He said nothing, letting the detective continue.

As he spoke, the police officer reached into an inside coat pocket and produced a photograph. "We have just received a reliable tip that this man, an underworld figure, is very likely in the Portland area." He held out the photo to Cotter. "This is Paul DeMosso, son of Joseph DeMosso, a gangland boss who was recently murdered in California. We think DeMosso's son may be here on some sort of reprisal mission directed at Edward Fusco.

"For a long time, we've been trying to connect Fusco to the DeMosso crew because of his relationship with Paul DeMosso's wife. But we haven't come up with any solid evidence. Now it looks as if Fusco may have been at odds with the family and is somehow involved in Joseph DeMosso's murder. It could be Paul DeMosso believes Fusco was behind the hit and is trying to prove it."

"Hit?" Nordie questioned. Both men turned to look at her. She had a distinct look of disbelief on her face. "That can't mean what I think it means. Not in Portland!"

Detective Hefflet nodded. He turned back to Cotter. "I don't want any gangland activity in my precinct. And I'm sure you don't, either. We've already shown this picture to your men who handle the Fusco route, but I want your students to see it, too. We'd like to know where DeMosso is, and what he's doing. Maybe they've seen him—or will."

Cotter had been watching the man's face. "My route men will do what they can, Ray. But I'm afraid the students will be heading back to Orono day after tomorrow. Their study is almost over." He looked down at the picture for the first time. "It's probably just as well that they're leaving. With this new development, I'd rather not have them involved in something so dangerous..." The words died away, and he squinted at the grainy black-and-white picture, unable to believe his eyes. The man had a mustache, but otherwise he looked familiar. "Ike Noonan," Cotter mumbled incredulously. His eyes shot to Detective Hefflet's. Slapping the picture with his other hand, he commanded in a low growl, "What the hell is going on? This man has been staying here for two weeks. Said he was a police detective. Called himself Noonan. Ike Noonan."

Ray bristled with surprise. "Living here?"

"Yes. We had an attempted break-in after his first visit. He suggested it might be an attempt to thwart some sort of investigation he was working on—something about embezzlement and prostitution—oh, what the hell difference does that make now." He ran a rough hand through his hair, frowning in thought. "Damn it! That was probably him—the bastard—faking a break-in just to have an excuse to hide out here."

"Could be. DeMosso is reputed to be ruthless and resourceful. And this is the place he'd want to be to find something incriminating against Fusco. Although what it might be, I can't guess."

Cotter berated himself harshly. "Damn it. Noonan—or DeMosso—showed me his police identification. It looked genuine."

"Probably was. Police get robbed, too." Detective Hefflet shrugged helplessly. "As I said, he's resourceful—"

"And ruthless?" Nordie stifled a cry, snatching the picture from Cotter's hand. "I don't believe it. Not Ike! He was so nice to Professor Webber. He liked her!"

Fear gripped Cotter like a vise as he remembered what Nordie had said earlier. Whirling toward his sister, he grabbed her shoulders. "Didn't you say he and Raine left together?"

Nordie's eyes were wide with terror, and her fingers trembled so badly the photo fell to the rug. A strangled cry escaped her throat. "She—she insisted...."

Cotter uttered an angry oath and turned to Ray Hefflet. "He's gone, and he took Professor Raine Webber with him—some kind of evidence. We thought they were going to headquarters."

Detective Hefflet's expression darkened to one of deep concern. "What did he find?"

Cotter's eyes cut back to Nordie. She was shaking her head. "I—I don't know. All I know is, as soon as Professor Webber found it, he was anxious to leave."

Hefflet shook his head. "If they found some link between Fusco and his father's murder, he's on his way to kill the man." He motioned toward the phone on Cotter's desk. "I'll need to notify headquarters."

Nordie put her hands to her temples, tears spilling down her cheeks. Her expression was desolate and frightened. "Oh, Cotter! It's all my fault!"

Cotter put a consoling arm around his sister's shoulders and turned to Detective Hefflet as he dialed. "This DeMosso. He won't hurt Raine?" It wasn't a question; it was a whispered prayer.

Detective Hefflet pursed his lips, shaking his head sadly, avoiding his host's eyes as he lifted the receiver. "DeMosso can't leave witnesses. I'm sorry, Mr. Hunt, but she could already be dead."

The thought hit Cotter like a physical blow. He sat back against his desk, running an unsteady hand through his hair. Raine? Dead? Raine Webber, custodian of the world's underdogs, heroically plucky, gentle-hearted Raine? He shook his head negating the idea, unable to picture the world deprived of such a giving woman. He realized, too, that he couldn't envision his own life going on, deprived of her quiet honesty.

The possibility that he might never see her again filled him with a sharp desolation he had never experienced before, not even after the death of his parents. "No!" He bolted up, heading for the door. "It can't be too late for us!"

Detective Hefflet had just finished his call. He hung up the phone, grabbing Cotter's arm. "You can't go. You're a civilian. Let us—"

Cotter jerked out of the officer's hold. "You do what you have to do, and so will I," he growled, never looking back.

Chapter Twelve

Cotter knew exactly where the Fusco residence was. Hadn't he himself suggested this area to Raine? He gritted his teeth in irritation, following Detective Hefflet's unmarked car. He had made no concessions to the officer, and he didn't plan to once they arrived at the Fusco residence. As they pulled past a large park, Detective Hefflet began to slow down. Cotter cursed at the delay, but then saw the need for reduced speed. The street had been blocked off from through traffic by a number of police cars.

Hefflet pulled over, and Cotter followed. Tearing open his door, he was immediately beside the officer. A uniformed policeman tried to detain him, but when Hefflet saw that Cotter was going to protest mightily, he raised a halting hand, "All right—" he shook his head "—let him pass, Rogers. He's with me."

As they moved toward the first row of cars, Detective Hefflet said, "This is as far as you go, Hunt.

There's nothing you can do, anyway, so stay low. We'll do our best to get her out."

"No, I have to go in," Cotter argued, bent on asserting his will.

Hefflet turned, his face stern. "Listen, Hunt. I've already gone way over the edge for you. You aren't going in. I promise you, if you set one foot beyond this point, I'll put you in protective custody." He looked down, pulling a gun from his shoulder holster. He then lifted a challenging brow toward Cotter. "That clear?"

Cotter looked discouraged but said nothing.

Someone with a bullhorn began to bellow to Cotter's left, and he quickly turned toward the house. An almost imperceptible movement of the curtains brought his whole body to attention. The amplified voice of the police lieutenant was demanding that DeMosso throw down his weapon, let Fusco and the woman go and give himself up. When there was no immediate response, the demands were repeated. Cotter swallowed, and he offered a silent prayer that in the next moment he would see Raine walk out safely.

The crack of gunfire dashed his hopes as DeMosso let go with his unquestionable answer. He intended to fight. Cotter raged, and Hefflet pulled him down behind the car. As several policemen returned fire, Cotter pressed a fist to his lips, stifling his urge to yell out to DeMosso, "Let her go, damn it! You owe us that." He slammed his knuckles into the side of the car in helpless frustration.

"Hey, man, take it easy." Hefflet cautioned in a rough whisper.

Cotter wrapped the throbbing fist with his other hand, growling, "What do you expect me to do? If she's still alive in there, one of your cops could kill her with a stray—"

An explosion tore through Cotter's biting words, and both men jerked around to see the dark sedan burst into flames.

"Looks like the gas tank got hit," Hefflet shouted.

Flames were lapping the sides of the car when Cotter heard a scream that seemed to be wrenched from the very depths of the dying car. Instantly, he knew it was Raine—knew she was in the burning vehicle.

Bolting up, oblivious to danger, he grabbed Detective Heffler by a shoulder. "She's in the trunk of DeMosso's car! Get me a crowbar!" His harsh face loomed over the man as he delivered the order.

"But—"

"Get it!" Cotter pulled the officer up bodily. "Now!"

It was a matter of seconds, but to Cotter, everything seemed to be moving in excruciatingly slow motion as the fire engulfed the car.

The instant the cold metal of the crowbar touched his hand, he started forward in a run. The sweat that beaded his face made him feel cold, but as soon as he got within ten feet of the car, his skin was struck with intense heat. He winced but pursued his task, desperately working the crowbar under the trunk.

His breathing was labored, and his heart was pounding like a wrecking ball against his ribs. It was not from the exertion of the run, he knew. But there was nothing he could do about the mindless terror that gripped him.

Fire. Scorching, blistering, killing fire. Before his eyes, instead of the car, he saw the old white house trailer. It was burning as it had been the night his parents had died. Again he felt the horror he'd known then, hearing his mother's screams as he'd carried Nordie, bundled in a blanket, from the inferno, and dragged a dazed Carl behind him. He relived his struggles, trying to run back in to rescue his mother and father, who were trapped behind a wall of flames in their bedroom, but being held back forcibly by two firemen. Their shouted warning came back to him in a rush. "No good, boy. Too late, too...late." By then the screams had died away. His parents were gone. And he? Forever after that night, he'd been sure it had been his cowardice that had killed them.

His brows formed a bridge of confusion over his eyes. Cowardice? No. He recalled it all now. He had tried to go back, tried to save his parents. It hadn't been his fear, after all, that had kept him from going in. He shook his head at the long-lost memory, repressed beneath the panic and tragedy of that terrible night. It had been the firemen who'd held him, struggling and fighting with all his strength, kept him from going back into the trailer.

Raine's screams filled the air around him, shattering the haunting memory, and once again the dark sedan blazed before him. Without a second thought he rammed the blade of the crowbar below the trunk's lock and jammed his body weight toward the ground.

There was a screech of metal and a loud pop as the trunk flew open. Smoke billowed out, burning Cotter's eyes as he reached in and scooped Raine into his arms and ran for cover toward the police car.

A bullet whizzed past his shoulder, and he flinched at the deadly whisper of sound. Barely able to see, eyes stinging, he stumbled. Clutching her close to him, he struggled to right himself. Just as he did, he felt hands pulling her from him.

"No!" he shouted. But even as he protested, she was lifted away, and he was dragged to safety behind the the police car and unceremoniously thrown to the ground.

A white-hot ball of fire lit up the sky, yielding the terrifying sound of disintegrating metal. The sedan had exploded, sending flaming debris flying. Cotter could hear pieces of metal crash into the exposed side of the car they were huddled behind, and he scrambled to cover Raine's body with his own.

He heard her moan and felt her body quake as she coughed. "Oh, Cotter," she rasped into his ear, "I thought—"

He quieted her, his fingers brushing her lips lightly. "Don't say it, Raine." He kissed her sooty cheek and smiled, relieved to feel her heart beating against his chest. Her face was nothing more than a blur. Still, it was the most beautiful sight he'd ever seen.

"Tear gas is goin' in!"

Raine lifted her gaze to the stranger who had spoken. She blinked several times to clear her vision. He was wearing a black suit and was crouched near her head. No doubt, a police detective. A uniformed officer, on the far side, was loading a gun.

Cotter carefully rolled off her but continued to shield her body with his. One arm remained draped protectively across her chest. She was surprised to feel his hand tremble as he gently touched her side. "Do you think you can sit up?" he asked quietly, his voice soft and full of concern.

"I—" She tried to rise but winced. "My hands are tied, Cotter."

His face hardened, and he lifted her gently to a sitting postion. "Lean on the car." He took her hands in his. "I'll get this untied."

She coughed again, her throat raw. Now she could feel the throbbing pain in her cheek where she'd rubbed and rubbed against the rough trunk carpet as she'd worked to dislodge her gag. After a brief moment, her hands were free. When she moved them to her lap, a groan welled in her throat. Her muscles had cramped and gone stiff from being held in an unnatural position.

"What is it?" Cotter asked, his voice tense with worry.

"Nothing. Just a cramp in my arm." She lifted tremulous lips in a small smile, looking up at his stern face. With her assurance, his features softened. Pulling her knees up, she began to unbuckle the belt that lashed them together.

"Let me." He covered her hands with his, halting her.

She could do nothing but stare at his obvious emotion. His eyes were saying things to her that her heart didn't dare believe. She loved him, but she feared she was reading something into his look of compassion that wasn't there. Finally, she willed herself to move her head, nodding her acquiescence.

As she rubbed her bruised wrists, Cotter tenderly unbuckled the leather belt that held her knees.

"He's coming out!" the black-suited detective informed them.

Cotter tossed the belt away and moved up beside her, rising to look toward the house through the car's rear window. Supported by his sturdy arm, she came shakily to her knees, squinting against the unaccustomed light.

She gasped behind a trembling hand as she saw the blond man she had known as Ike Noonan stumble out, coughing and waving his hands.

Cotter put an arm around her shoulder but said nothing.

A flurry of activity and he was handcuffed, in the custody of several police officers. As he was led past Cotter and Raine he dragged his escorts to a halt and looked directly at Raine, his mouth twisting in an unreadable half smile.

She met his gaze squarely, asking, "Did you kill him?"

He snorted, shaking his head. "He beat me to it. Took pills last night, the coward." He smiled knowingly. "Didn't leave a note."

She breathed a sigh. "You couldn't have done it anyway, Ike. You didn't kill me." She reached out to touch his sleeve. "You couldn't have done it."

"Enough," he barked, breaking eye contact. In a commanding tone he addressed the officers who held his arms. "Let's get out of here. I want to call my wife."

COTTER PUSHED OPEN the front door of his house and stepped back to let Raine precede him. "We're home," he said, sounding subdued. He had been quiet ever since Paul DeMosso had given himself up, and she wondered why his mood had changed from an almost loving relief to this somber melancholy. She felt his hand slide around her shoulders in a protective gesture as Detective Hefflet entered.

They all stopped short to see Nordie and her entourage of male students sitting expectantly, two to a step, on the curved staircase. Nordie leapt to her feet. "Thank goodness you're all right!" She paused, her mouth gaping. "What happened to your faces?"

Raine smiled. It hurt a little. She was sure that her rug-burned cheek and Cotter's reddened skin made them a sight to behold. "We're all right, really."

"Actually, we're medium rare," Cotter's grin was twisted and didn't reflect any happiness in his eyes.

Raine explained. "The glow you see is from an antiseptic ointment."

"Oh. Good. I thought you'd been basted." Nordie sagged, clutching the banister with relief. "That exploding car was all over the news—you two are famous. The 'unidentified professor held hostage was rescued spectacularly—by her husband—just before the car exploded,'' Nordie quoted, shaking her head and laughing nervously. "First media marriage on record. Congratulations."

Detective Hefflet broke in to explain, "The department wanted to protect your identities, but it doesn't look like it'll be necessary now. The word is, DeMosso's working a deal. Last I heard, he had the cops in two states, and the feds in Washington, jumping through hoops doing his bidding." He flicked his eyes from Cotter to Raine. "The man's no fool. Looks like he may turn state's evidence—and with what he knows, it's my guess he'll get whatever deal he asks for. New identity, for sure. He's blown away, otherwise." He shrugged. "DeMosso will talk, and while heads are rolling, he'll disappear into federal protection."

Raine was surprised at this turn of events, and something deep inside of her blossomed in a vague sort of happiness. It was strange, considering what Paul DeMosso had put her through, but somehow, she couldn't bring herself to hate him. A bit haltingly, she asked, "What about his family?"

Detective Hefflet plugged his suit pockets with his hands. "I heard his wife and children have already been taken into protective custody. They're moving fast. That's a fact."

Raine sighed, feeling very tired. "Paul DeMosso may land on his feet in this thing after all." She exhaled slowly. "I guess I don't need to worry about him." She gave Nordie and the young men a tired smile. "Right now, I'm just grateful to see everybody again. For a while, I didn't know if I would."

Nordie clasped her hands together, looking pained. "Oh! I didn't, either. You can't believe how many of my sins passed before my eyes when I saw that car explode! I made a vow that if I ever saw you again, no matter into how much trouble it got me, I'd spill my guts to you about every nasty thing I've done!"

Cotter interrupted quietly, "I don't think she has the strength to hear about everything, Nordie."

She waved his argument aside, rushing on. "I can't help it! Its guts-spilling time." She cast a glance back at the quiet, waiting students, who were watching her expectantly. "And I want you all to hear this, too. Everyone should know what an awful person I am." She clutched her blouse theatrically. "I, alone, decided to tell Professor Webber that Cotter was gay. And then I, alone, took it upon myself to tell Cotter that I'd told her that flagrant untruth. Naturally, he was furious with me, but because he loves me—even though I don't deserve it—he didn't give me away!"

She looked pleadingly at Raine, who looked astonished. "I didn't do it to hurt anybody. Actually, it was so you would notice Carl, and pay attention to him. Help him recover. I hope you understand."

When Raine didn't answer immediately, she hurried on, "And then, when Anona showed up, it was my idea to say she was a psychiatrist. Not Cotter's." She put a supporting hand on Bill's head as she gingerly nudged a knee between him and George and stepped down to the marble entry. Walking toward Raine, she added sheepishly, "I didn't mean to hurt anybody. It's just my oddball sense of humor." She swallowed, chewing on her lower lip. "I should have admitted it long ago, but I'm such a spoiled coward, I—I just—" she smiled weakly "—didn't." Looking pitiful and humble, she cast her eyes down and, with a tremor in her voice, whispered, "Fail me, professor. It's all I deserve."

Cotter grunted. Squeezing Raine's shoulder, he added sardonically, "Be careful. She's damn good at this."

Nordie's head bobbed up, her eyes flashing with spirit. "Cotter Hunt! I meant that. Every word came from my heart. I'm asking Professor Webber to forgive me. Don't tease."

Raine lifted a hand to Nordie's shoulder. "I believe you." She shook her head. "You couldn't make up such a story. You're an imp, but I can't be angry with you for long." She dropped her hand and smiled at the younger woman. "You're forgiven. And I won't fail you."

When Nordie smiled, Cotter cautioned, "Don't feel too smug, little sister. Tonight I saw her forgive a man who almost killed her." Raine turned to look at him. His expression was unreadable, but she thought she had sensed a certain tension in his words.

"Well, in that case, did I mention that I also locked you two in the wine cellar and turned off the elect—"

"Maybe you'd better quit while you're ahead," Cotter interrupted.

Raine's eyes flickered back to Nordie. Her mind was a jumble of new facts. With Nordie's admission, she'd discovered that Cotter had been as much the victim in this as she. If only he hadn't made love to her and then regretted it so completely. If only that could be as easily explained away as all the other things.

"Ahem." Detective Hefflet cleared his throat, drawing everyone's attention. "Guess I'll be going." He nodded toward the group.

Cotter's arm slid from Raine's shoulders as he moved to open the door. "Good night, Ray. And thanks for escorting us to and from the hospital."

"Hospital?" Nordie asked, her voice high.

Cotter held up his left arm. A three-inch strip of gauze was wrapped around it just above the wrist. "I got a little more than medium rare in places."

Nordie's eyes narrowed. "Yeah, I've been meaning to ask you about your mad dash into the flames. I thought you had a thing about fire. And here you go and pull Professor Webber out of a sizzling inferno a millisecond before it becomes a bomb with seat covers." She crossed her arms. "How would you explain that? Temporary insanity?"

Raine caught on the phrase "a thing about fires." Yes, she remembered now. Cotter had told her once that he was afraid of fire. She'd forgotten all about it. She turned to look up at him, her expression inquiring.

"Yes, well..." He inclined his head toward the stairs. "Why don't you all go get ready for dinner. Raine and I have a lot to discuss."

Nordie's grin was devilish. "What to discuss?"

Cotter gave her a push. "My insanity." He motioned to the boys. "A couple of you take her away—maybe to Boise, Idaho."

HE TOOK HER HAND and led her out onto the beach. A cool breeze ruffled her hair, and she breathed deeply. Though she tried to concentrate on the scenery, she couldn't draw her mind away from Cotter. Feeling strangely nervous, she wondered why he had brought her out here. His resonant voice startled her now. "Why don't you take off your shoes?" he suggested, sitting down on the sand and removing his suede oxfords and socks.

Her eyes darted to his face, and he met her curious gaze with an uneasy frown. He lifted a hand to take hers. "Join me?" Allowing him to help her, she sat down beside him, pulling off her sandals. When she noticed he was rolling up his slacks, she asked. "Are we going clamming?"

He shook his head, looking very solemn. "No, just walking. The feel of sand and water on bare feet is calming. We need that."

"I agree." She nodded, rolling her cotton slacks to midcalf. When she had finished, he helped her to her feet and they began to walk again. Raine was surprised at how pleasant the water felt as it lapped around her feet and ankles. In the past month, the ocean had become less threatening, and she smiled at the realization.

"What's funny?" Cotter's voice was so close it startled her.

She met his troubled gaze. "Nothing, really." She kicked at the surf thoughtfully. "I just realized I'm not afraid of the ocean anymore."

He took her elbow. "You're not afraid of much anymore, are you?"

She thought about that. "Maybe."

"Maybe?" His brow arched. "Come, now. You've taken on everything from clams to criminals, and won. What could you still be afraid of?"

Her attention shifted to the sand. The squirt of a clam near her bare toes brought back a warm flash of memory, Cotter holding her and kissing her, the day they'd gone clamming. She remembered vividly her frustration. That same night, after the attempted break-in, their lovemaking had been supreme, until he told her of his unwillingness to let himself love her.

And now he was asking her what she was afraid of. How could she tell him that it was him she feared, her unreasonable love for a man frightened her more than bullets. She shook her head, deciding to be vague. "One or two...things."

"Hmm." He was silent for a long moment before changing the subject abruptly. "I couldn't believe it when you actually smiled at Paul DeMosso tonight—after everything he'd done to you. You still forgave him, didn't you?"

Completely taken off guard by Cotter's remark, she squinted at his profile. There was a definite edge to his words now. She was sure of it. Stopping in her tracks, she turned to face him. "Of course I did."

He stopped, too, turning to look down at her through guarded lids. "That's what I thought."

Raine could see no calm in the darkness of his eyes. She wasn't sure of what she saw there, but it was anything but peaceful. His handsome features grew more troubled as he admitted, "I didn't know you cared so much—about him. Even after he used you, used the project, almost killed you? You must really have loved him."

Raine was stunned. Loved? Paul DeMosso? Looking back on how Paul took it when he found out his own wife conspired to kill his father, she could feel nothing but pity for the man.

She cringed at the sight of despair in Cotter's eyes as he watched her. Was it pity? The last emotion she wanted to draw from Cotter was pity. But of course, that was what she saw in the endless darkness of his gaze. Did he really believe she loved a criminal who had used her and threatened her life? Good Lord! How wrong could one man be? But she couldn't tell him the truth—that it was Cotter she really loved.

She abruptly turned away. She mumbled, "I'd rather not talk about this, if you don't mind." Blindly, she stumbled away. The wet sand weighted her bare feet, making her progress seem awkward and slow.

Cotter caught up with her, taking her wrist. "This has to be said."

"No, it doesn't." She shrugged out of his grasp, casting her gaze out over the ocean to keep from meeting his probing eyes. It was hard to have the man she loved questioning her about another man. "I'd rather sort everything out alone," she pleaded. With a grim determination to get away, she hurried down the beach.

Hands on her shoulders turned her around. "Raine, talk to me." It was a plea, this time, not an order. He swallowed. "You forgave Ike. You forgave Nordie." The shadow of the haunted animal loomed in his eyes as he asked huskily, "Can't you forgive me, too?"

The starkness of his words sent a shiver down her spine. "Forgive you?" For his using her—for making love to her? Why? To soothe his feelings of guilt? Hardly hearing her own words she told him, "You used me badly, Cotter, in a way no other human being ever has."

His tanned face seemed to drain of all color. But his eyes, direct and dark, pulled her gaze back to him. "I know. But won't you let me at least explain?" Wounded, she shook her head to deny his request, but he continued in a deep, husky tone, "Well, professor, I'm going to tell you anyway, because it's something I've never told any woman before."

"I don't want to hear this!" she moaned, resolutely pressing her fists against his chest, intent on pulling away.

They halted, and his arms encircled her, hugging her to him. "No, you're going to hear me out." His voice was determined. "I was a fool. I didn't want love or friendship or responsibility for other people. I lied to myself for a long time. Made excuses. But I found out tonight, when I heard you scream, that there's just one thing harder to take than losing people I've loved and felt responsible for, and that is never giving myself the chance to love—and knowing it was my own fault.

"When I thought I'd lost you, Raine, I died." With his hands framing her face, he lifted her head so that her gaze met his. "Raine," he went on in a subdued whisper, "maybe it's too late for you to forgive me. I hope not. More than anything in the world, I wish you'd give me another chance."

"Another chance?" she breathed.

"Yes. Because I love you." His breath was feathering her hair, and she could feel the rapid beating of his heart. "Raine—" His voice broke in a touching display of vulnerability, and she cherished his genuine emotion. He was whispering, "I know you cared for Ike. I know he hurt you and I know I've hurt you, too." He ran long fingers though her hair. "But I was wrong before. I'm one stray who wants very badly to be accepted by you. I'll do whatever it takes."

She looked up at him. His mouth was only a breath away from hers. "What do you mean?" she asked breathlessly.

"I mean my intentions are honorable." His eyes glittered into hers with a magnificent intensity that made her heart soar. His smile was softer than she had ever remembered. "I should have realized how I felt about you when I couldn't keep my hands off you."

She felt tears prick her eyelids and could only gaze wordlessly at him as he went on.

"I love you Raine. I want to marry you."

Her eyes widened as she stared through tear-spangled lashes at his face, basking in the warmth she saw there. "You're proposing...marriage?"

He kissed her softly, murmuring against her cheek. "You're a treasure, and I can't lose you now that I've found you."

She wanted to believe him more than she wanted the breath of life, but she had to ask, "And Anona?"

He brushed a loving kiss across her lips, then pulled away reluctantly. The frustrated sound in his throat echoed her own distress at being deprived of his touch. Taking her hand, he began to walk with her again. "Anona is attractive. She'll find someone." In one quick, unexpected motion, he turned back to face Raine, his eyes black, penetrating. A surge of emotion too strong to ignore seemed to take hold of him, and he encircled her with strong, protective arms, rasping against her cheek, "Raine, please agree to marry me."

She blinked. He was holding her blessedly close, breathing against her ear. Of course she would marry him. There was little to forgive. And now that she also knew that he had been as drawn into their lovemaking as she, all her doubts were dispelled. "I—" Her voice cracked and she swallowed, intent on trying again, when something caught her eye.

A green patch, all but hidden between two sand dunes, jogged her memory. It was the wild cranberry bed. A flutter of excitement made her heart race. Working hard at keeping her voice even, she said, "I can't wait that long."

Her eyes moved meaningfully to the thick mat of green vines. When she lifted her head to find his eyes again, her lips were curved upward in a direct, seductive smile. "I've loved you—only you—for so long, I want to..." She paused, reclining and pulling him down beside her. In a throaty whisper, she finished, "I want to love you, now."

"You love me?" The question was hesitant, as if he were almost afraid to believe it.

She lifted her cheek to nuzzle his chin. "Only you."

His lips found hers as he swept her into his arms and down to their fragrant mattress. His mouth moved across hers hungrily, and she gloried in the fiery sensations his touch released within her. "But, when," he murmured against an upturned corner of her mouth, "will you marry me?"

She framed his magnificent head in her hands. "I'll call my parents when we get back to the house. As soon as they can get here we'll be married. Is that all right?"

"Tell them to fly. I don't want you to have time to take in any more strays." His voice held a teasing note; his breath mingled with hers.

A laugh bubbled in her throat as he lowered her to the blossoming bed, and within moments they were one, entwined in a passion that ignited their bodies. Together, they shared a priceless treasure.

Epilogue

Raine shook the snow from her hair and handed her coat to Hanna. "Where is..." The words died away as she heard the familiar strains of an up-tempo jazz standard drifting from the den. "Never mind, Hanna." With a light heart, she hurried toward the sound. She'd just returned from an overnight trip to Orono—her first night away from Cotter since their marriage in July. Right now, she wanted nothing more than to see Cotter and hold him in her arms. Without knocking she pushed the double doors open to find him sitting quietly in the dark, listening to their favorite music.

When she entered, he turned, and from the light in the hallway, she could see his features open in a smile. "Hello, darling." He stood up and walked to her. Pushing the doors closed, he took her into his arms. His scent filled her head, making her feel dizzy with happiness, and she leaned into his warmth for support.

"I missed you last night," he murmured.

Lifting her head reluctantly from his chest, she smiled into his eyes. "Me, too." She took his hand and led him toward the couch. "Come and sit with me while we talk. Oh, by the way, on the radio I heard that Paul DeMosso's evidence has brought seventy-two indictments of underworld figures and uncovered a powerful organized crime network operating across the United States—drug trafficking, car theft—"

He stopped short, halting her. "I read about it in this evening's paper and called Detective Hefflet. He told me DeMosso's gone—spirited away—the whole family, too. Even his wife. That surprises me, considering what she did."

Raine lifted a shoulder. "Not me. He wouldn't have made the deal without Doria. He really loves her."

Cotter's eyes glistened in the darkness, and as her eyes adjusted, she could see that he was smiling. "I guess when you put it that way, I understand." His voice was gentle, loving. "Anyway, I knew you'd want to know, so I found out for you. Now, could you do something for me?"

She slanted her head questioningly. "Sure. What?"

"Let's not talk about him anymore." His smile had faded slightly. He seemed cautious, almost uncomfortable."

Raine inhaled deeply, shaking her head. The marvel of their love still filled her with awe. Pulling up on tiptoes, she kissed him. "The subject is closed."

He relaxed visibly and chuckled, nuzzling her glasses askew on her face. "Thanks."

"Cotter..." A laugh bubbled in her throat as she pushed the new frames back into place. "Whatever happened to the old saying about boys never making passes at girls who wear glasses?"

He pulled the gold frames off her nose and slipped them into his jacket pocket. "Trashed. Kiss me." He growled the command playfully, nipping at her lips and pressing her down until she was arched precariously backward.

She cautioned, "We're going to fall."

He kissed her throat and teased, "I already have. Let's go to bed."

He gave her an urgent yet playful caress that made her body begin to tingle with need. It still amazed her how quickly he could bring her to this yearning state of desire. But even as she encircled his neck with her arms, she tried to think clearly. "Isn't your brother's family due to get here soon for dinner?"

Cotter stopped his nuzzling and lifted his face just enough to peer into her eyes. "Is it Christmas Eve already?"

She smiled up into his laughing eyes. "I'm afraid so. Merry Christmas."

"That means Nordie'll be here any minute, too. Who's she bringing this time—a group of underground radicals working on heat-seeking missiles? Probably blow up our bedroom sometime tonight."

Raine couldn't restrain her laughter. "No heat-seeking radicals. Just someone named Gregor, I think."

He looked down at her, his long lashes hooding the twinkle of fun that always seemed to brighten his eyes lately. "Gregor?" He shook his head doubtfully. "Here we go again."

Raine closed her eyes, enjoying the softness of his cashmere sweater against her face. "So, Nordie's changed majors again."

"Naturally." Raine stepped away from his arms, her desire to curl up in his lap now very strong. In a throaty whisper, she suggested, "Come. Sit on the couch with me." She laced her fingers in his as she took up the thread of their conversation. "This time, I think she's found her calling—as a performing arts major."

"As a performing arts major, maybe. I don't actually see her graduating." He allowed her to lead him to the couch. As he sat down he pulled her to him. "What did they say at the university. Are you going to get the extended anthropology project?"

She snuggled into the crook of his arm, nodding. "That's the good news. Not only do they want me to head up a more extensive project from here, they've also authorized me to hire an assistant." She turned happy, shining eyes at her expectant husband. "Remember George?"

He pursed his lips. "George? Wasn't he the kid who was in love with you?"

Startled, she denied it. "Heavens, no! Whatever gave you that idea?"

She felt him shift, his smile becoming enigmatic. He patted her knee. "Never mind. Maybe he cries at all weddings. Now, what's the bad news?"

She dropped her eyes to his hand as it caressed her knee. "The bad news is they're sending up four students right after the new year—for a month. January and June will be the seminar months when students come up here."

His laugh was hearty. "Only four?"

She nodded but didn't smile. "That's four too many, if you ask me." She looked away, out the window. Large, wet flakes were fluttering down, turning the point in the distance a picture-perfect, glistening white. Quietly, she added, "They're all young women."

He was silent for a moment before she felt a finger on her chin, turning her to face him. "So?"

She shrugged. "I'm not sure I want four women trailing you for a month."

"I've got an idea." His grin was wide and rakish. "Why don't we tell them I'm gay?"

Knowing what she now knew about him, she burst out laughing at the outrageous idea. "And how would we explain me—the sleep-in therapist?"

His smile was tender. "Why don't we let George take care of the girls. He needs the practice." Dismissing the subject, he hugged her to him and whispered in her ear. "Let's go to bed. I'll have Hanna tell the family we'll be down later."

She hid her smile. "Cotter, this is your niece's first visit. Oh, and Cammie told me the doctor is very optimistic about Carl. The therapy seems to be effective."

He nodded. "That is good news, but—" he leaned near, kissing her cheek and whispering seductively "—I want to love you, Raine. We could join them for dessert."

She twisted in his arms to face him, pulling her feet up beneath her. With a sigh of contentment she offered a compromise. "Let's have dinner with them and then I'll send everybody home early. After all, it's Christmas Eve."

She went on whispering, "Cotter, we just have time to change. Don't you want to taste the cranberry sauce I made—" She hushed him with a hand to his lips, finishing, "—With cranberries from our wild cranberry patch?"

"Later." He was unbuttoning her blouse, kissing the softly rising flesh beneath her lacy bra.

She couldn't help responding. Head lolled back, her body began to pulsate with heightened desire. "Oh, Cotter..." she moaned contentedly. "You're insatiable."

"I know." He slipped a hand to the back of her neck, stroking her softness there. His tongue explored further, but she tried again, her voice less resolute, a tremulous whisper. "And the special wine—from the cellar..." He suckled a rosy peak, and she gave in, sighing.

He was moving down, kissing the slight roundness of her stomach, murmuring, "You're sweeter than any wine."

She felt her slacks open at his touch and gasped. "What if Hanna comes in?"

"She'll knock," he assured her, his voice deep with promise. Warm, loving hands slid down, enveloping her. She lowered her eyes to the silver glimmer of his hair. Her whole world was this man. His touch was magic, making her forget everything and everyone else. Wetting trembling lips, she curled her fingers in his thick hair, a delighted smile lifting her lips. Dinner would be late.

WORLDWIDE LIBRARY IS YOUR TICKET TO ROMANCE, ADVENTURE AND EXCITEMENT

Experience it all in these big, bold Bestsellers— Yours exclusively from WORLDWIDE LIBRARY WHILE QUANTITIES LAST

To receive these Bestsellers, complete the order form, detach and send together with your check or money order (include 75¢ postage and handling), payable to WORLDWIDE LIBRARY, to:

In the U.S.
WORLDWIDE LIBRARY
Box 52040
Phoenix, AZ
85072-2040

In Canada
WORLDWIDE LIBRARY
P.O. Box 2800, 5170 Yonge Street
Postal Station A, Willowdale, Ontario
M2N 6J3

Quant.	Title	Price
	WILD CONCERTO, Anne Mather	$2.95
	A VIOLATION, Charlotte Lamb	$3.50
	SECRETS, Sheila Holland	$3.50
	SWEET MEMORIES, LaVyrle Spencer	$3.50
	FLORA, Anne Weale	$3.50
	SUMMER'S AWAKENING, Anne Weale	$3.50
	FINGER PRINTS, Barbara Delinsky	$3.50
	DREAMWEAVER, Felicia Gallant/Rebecca Flanders	$3.50
	EYE OF THE STORM, Maura Seger	$3.50
	HIDDEN IN THE FLAME, Anne Mather	$3.50
	ECHO OF THUNDER, Maura Seger	$3.95
	DREAM OF DARKNESS, Jocelyn Haley	$3.95

YOUR ORDER TOTAL	$_____
New York and Arizona residents add appropriate sales tax	$_____
Postage and Handling	$ .75
I enclose	$_____

NAME _____

ADDRESS _____ APT.# _____

CITY _____

STATE/PROV. _____ ZIP/POSTAL CODE _____

WW3

She fought for a bold future until she could no longer ignore the...

ECHO OF THUNDER

MAURA SEGER

Author of **Eye of the Storm**

ECHO OF THUNDER is the love story of James Callahan and Alexis Brockton, who forge a union that must withstand the pressures of their own desires and the challenge of building a new television empire.

Author Maura Seger's writing has been described by *Romantic Times* as having a "superb blend of historical perspective, exciting romance and a deep and abiding passion for the human soul."

Available in SEPTEMBER or reserve your copy for August shipping by sending your name, address and zip or postal code, along with a cheque or money order for—$4.70 (includes 75¢ for postage and handling) payable to Worldwide Library Reader Service to:

Worldwide Library Reader Service

In the U.S.:
Box 52040,
Phoenix, Arizona,
85072-2040

In Canada:
5170 Yonge Street, P.O. Box 2800,
Postal Station A,
Willowdale, Ontario, M2N 6J3

EYE OF THE STORM

MAURA SEGER

A powerful portrayal of the events of World War II in the Pacific, *Eye of the Storm* is a riveting story of how love triumphs over hatred. In this, the first of a three-book chronicle, Army nurse Maggie Lawrence meets Marine Sgt. Anthony Gargano. Despite military regulations against fraternization, they resolve to face together whatever lies ahead.... Author Maura Seger, also known to her fans as Laurel Winslow, Sara Jennings, Anne MacNeil and Jenny Bates, was named 1984's Most Versatile Romance Author by *The Romantic Times*.

At your favorite bookstore now or send your name, address and zip or postal code, along with a check or money order for $4.25 (includes 75¢ for postage and handling) payable to Worldwide Library Reader Service to:

WORLDWIDE LIBRARY READER SERVICE
In the U.S.:
Box 52040,
Phoenix, AZ 85072-2040

In Canada:
5170 Yonge Street,
P.O. Box 2800,
Postal Station A,
Willowdale, Ont. M2N 6J3

Take 4 books & a surprise gift FREE

SPECIAL LIMITED-TIME OFFER

Mail to **Harlequin Reader Service**®

In the U.S.
2504 West Southern Ave.
Tempe, AZ 85282

In Canada
P.O. Box 2800, Station "A"
5170 Yonge Street
Willowdale, Ontario M2N 6J3

YES! Please send me 4 free Harlequin American Romance® novels and my free surprise gift. Then send me 4 brand-new novels as they come off the presses. Bill me at the low price of $2.25 each — a 11% saving off the retail price. There are no shipping, handling or other hidden costs. There is no minimum number of books I must purchase. I can always return a shipment and cancel at any time. Even if I never buy another book from Harlequin, the 4 free novels and the surprise gift are mine to keep forever.

Name _____ (PLEASE PRINT)

Address _____ Apt. No. _____

City _____ State/Prov. _____ Zip/Postal Code _____

This offer is limited to one order per household and not valid to present subscribers. Price is subject to change.

DOAR—SUB—1

Just what the woman on the go needs!
BOOKMATE

The perfect "mate" for all Harlequin paperbacks!

Holds paperbacks open for hands-free reading!

- TRAVELING
- VACATIONING
- AT WORK • IN BED
- COOKING • EATING
- STUDYING

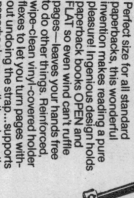

Snaps closed for easy carrying.

Perfect size for all standard paperbacks, this wonderful invention makes reading a pure pleasure! Ingenious design holds paperback books OPEN and FLAT so even wind can't ruffle pages—leaves your hands free to do other things. Reinforced, wipe-clean vinyl-covered holder flexes to let you turn pages without undoing the strap...supports paperbacks so well, they have the strength of hardcovers!

Available now. Send your name, address, and zip or postal code, along with a check or money order for just $4.99 + .75¢ for postage & handling (for a total of $5.74) payable to Harlequin Reader Service to:

Harlequin Reader Service

In the U.S.
2504 West Southern Avenue
Tempe, AZ 85282

In Canada
P.O. Box 2800, Postal Station A
5170 Yonge Street,
Willowdale, Ont. M2N 6J3

MATE-1R